THE
SARAH
BOOK
SCOTT
McCLANAHAN

Tyrant Books
9 Clinton St
Upper North Store
NY, NY 10002

Via Piagge Marine 23
Sezze (LT) 04018
Italy

www.NYTyrant.com

Cover design by Erik Carter
Page design by Adam Robinson

For Julia

Portions of this book have been plagiarized

PART ONE

There is only one thing I know about life. If you live long enough you start losing things. Things get stolen from you: First you lose your youth, and then your parents, and then you lose your friends, and finally you end up losing yourself.

I was the best drunk driver in the world. I'd been doing it for years. One morning Sarah came home from work and went back to bed. I tucked her in tight and kissed her forehead and told her not to worry about a thing. I told her to drift off to dreamland and not worry about her night shift and everything would be better when she woke up. Then I shut the door behind me and snuck down the stairs. I dodged the piles of basement junk and walked to a tiny room where we kept the out of tune piano from Sarah's childhood. This is where I kept the big bottle. I took out my empty water bottle from my back pocket and then I opened up the piano top. The wood creaked eek and popped open like a monster's mouth. "I'm worried about you," Sarah told me a few weeks before. I thought about that now as I reached inside the open upright piano and pulled out the bottle. The piano keys tickled out a tune as I twisted off the bottle top and held the empty water bottle up to it and filled the water bottle full. I listened to its love song. I screwed both lids back on tight and then I put the big bottle back and shut the piano top shut.

It was time for my favorite part. It was time to drive. I drove down the street and through red lights and stop signs shouting stop. I zipped alongside cars at seventy miles an hour and thought, "We're all just a few feet from one another. We're all just a few feet from finding out the physics of death."

Sometimes I said this stuff out loud and sometimes I didn't. I slipped onto the interstate and watched the white lines pass and remembered my friend who used to laugh like a maniac when I got in the car and shouted, "I'm the best drunk driver in the world" and then hit the gas. And you know what, he was right. It was like his reflexes were improved or something. Or it was like he wasn't all tense and nervous and could drive like he wasn't driving. I asked him once what his secret was to never getting pulled over and he told me to be invisible. I whispered this wisdom now, "Be invisible, Scott. Be invisible."

I drank from the water bottle full of gin and I chased it with water from another water bottle and then I did it again. I reached down into the glove box and pulled out the mouthwash. I popped the top and giggled once and gargled it down. Then I drove towards the blue sky and the purple mountain majesty and spit the mouthwash back into the mouth wash bottle. I listened to the radio and I looked for a CD and I felt what I never felt. I felt calm and I felt glowing and I felt invisible. And so I drove up the interstate hill. Invisible. Then I heard Iris talking.

"Oh shit," I said. I'd forgotten about the kids. I looked into the back seat and there was my son Sam and there was my daughter Iris sitting in the backseat. I was always doing stupid shit like bringing the kids along and forgetting about this or doing shit like putting the kids in the car and not even knowing I was putting the kids in the car. I shouted now, "You guys alright back there? You all just sit back and enjoy the drive. Maybe we'll go over to Grandma and Grandpa's. You want to go to Grandma and Grandpa's?"

They did. I threw my arm in the air and shouted: "Let's go to Grandma's." The kids laughed in the backseat and so I shouted it again, "Let's go to Grandma's," except this time they didn't laugh. But I didn't care. I wasn't going to let them ruin my day with their grumpiness. So I took a sip of gin again and then I chased it with water again and I saw the whole world go wild. I saw how nervous I was every day that Sarah was going to catch my bottles. I saw how nervous I was Sarah was going to find my hiding spots. And so I drank it down. I imagined myself drinking all of the skin of the world and all of the blood of the world and the spirits of all my friends and I was drinking the air. I was melting my children and I was drinking them too. And they tasted great.

I kept driving to Grandma's and that's when I saw a cop car parked beside the road. Shit. Shit. Hit the brakes. Hit the brakes. Speed gun. We passed the cop. I looked up in the rear view mirror and I thought, "Don't move. Please." I imagined myself invisible. Then I saw the cop car inch forward and then pull out onto the interstate. I saw the cop car lights flip on and start flashing. Red. Blue. White. Red. Blue. White. I drove for a moment and then I remembered my neighbor the cop who told me one time, "It's what people do after they get pulled over that gets them arrested." I slowed down and pulled alongside the road just a few feet from the cars whipping past us at 70 MPH. We were all so close to killing one another, always. The cop car pulled behind me. I watched him in the rear view.

He sat in his cop car for a second and so I reached into my shirt pocket and pulled out three pieces of gum I always kept in there. I popped them in my mouth to help cover up my smell and I watched the state trooper stand up out of his car and then he kept standing up more and even more until he stood tall. He walked tall towards me and I watched him touch the back of my car to leave his fingerprints in case I shot him and drove away. I rolled the window down and the cop said, "License and registration please."

But I was ready for him already. I always kept my license and registration and proof of insurance in the passenger seat so if I was ever pulled over I wouldn't go stumbling all drunk through the glove box looking for them. I reached for it now and kept repeating inside my head, "Don't shake. Please don't shake." I always sat in parking lots when I was drinking and practiced talking without slurring my words or shaking my hands. But now here I was and my words were slurring and my hands were shaking too. I was barely able to hand him my stuff without dropping it. The cop didn't say anything. He bent over and looked in the car.

Then he stood beside the car and looked at my registration. He looked at my license. He looked at my proof of insurance. And then he leaned over a little bit like he smelled something on me. I was sure he could smell it. The kids kicked and talked to themselves in the back seat.

"Just a second," he said and walked back to the police car and sat down. It was finally over and Sarah was going to know. Iris and Sam started crying a little bit.

"It's okay guys," I said. "Everything is fine."

But I knew it wasn't. I saw him coming back and asking me, "Sir, have you had any alcohol today?" And then, "Would you please get out of your vehicle for me?" I saw Sarah coming to the police station to get the kids and I imagined child protective services showing up and questioning her. I would cry when I told her what happened and how I lied all the time and how I put the children in danger and how I was destroying the life we made together. I would tell her how I was destroying our lives.

And so I watched him finally get out of his car and walk back to mine. I waited for him to ask me, "Sir, would you get out of your car?" But he didn't. He handed me back everything I had handed him just a few minutes before. Then he looked in the backseat and instead of arresting me, he said, "Well, hello kiddos. Will you guys help me make sure Daddy doesn't go too fast today?"

I took the license and registration and the proof of insurance. The kids didn't say anything back.

And so he walked away. And I wasn't caught. I was too afraid to say thank you. The children were actually crying now. Snot was running out of their noses. I said, "Babies don't you cry," but my words were so slurred you couldn't even understand them. I reached to change the CD playing but my hands were shaking so bad I finally just stopped. I pulled back on the interstate and drove on and I smiled and started to weave between the lanes on the interstate lines. I smiled and listened to the children cry and I felt the world glow. I threw up in a plastic bag from Walmart and I threw it out the window. The children were still crying, but I didn't care now. I was free and I wasn't caught and I was driving our death car so fast and unafraid. I was destroying our lives now and it felt so fucking wonderful.

A few weeks later, I burned this Bible. I looked over at my friend Chris and said, "Hey man we should burn a Bible." Of course, we'd been fucking around like this for a while now. A month before we were going through the Taco Bell drive thru and our order total came up 6.66. So every time I went out with friends and wanted to freak them out, I'd start talking about how I felt the devil was after me. I'd say, "Like seriously, I think the fucking devil is after me." Then I'd stop at Taco Bell and order my devil order and it'd come up 6.66 just like always and everyone would go holy fuck and lose their shit.

Maybe this was a sign. Maybe Satan was trying to tell me something.

So I started looking for a Bible to burn. Chris thought it wasn't a good idea and that Sarah was going to find out. I told him not to worry about Sarah. I was a grown-ass man and if I wanted to burn a Bible then Sarah couldn't tell me not to.

I looked through the basement bookshelves and at all the Bibles we owned. There were three of them. There was a Bible from the Gideon's and there was a Bible with a black cover that had been my childhood Bible. Then there was another Bible on the bottom shelf. This was the newest Bible. This was the Bible someone got us for our wedding.

I reached down and pulled it off the shelf. It was one of those big plush white Bibles and it had Sarah and Scott McClanahan on the corner in gold. It's the kind of Bible you see on people's coffee tables or at somebody's Grandma's house. "I don't think we should," Chris said, but I didn't listen to him. So I put the Bible on the table and opened it to the book of Daniel. *He ordered the furnace heated seven times hotter than usual.* I walked over to another part of the basement where Sarah kept her father's old tools. I looked around for a while and then I finally found some old lighter fluid and matches.

I took the lighter fluid and squirted squirt squirt on the Bible pages and then I took a match and it lit. Then I blew the match out. "O shit. Let me do something." I turned off the lights.

Chris repeated, "We shouldn't be doing this. We shouldn't be doing this."

But I just lit another match and let the match drop drown on the Bible and then there was a ripping sound and the Bible blazed bright.

My face glowed in light. I saw myself in the reflection from the window and there was a halo around my head.

The flames spread across the pages like ocean waves and then burned from red to brown to black. I put out the bits of dark embers and that was it. Nothing happened. It was the same as when I drank in the car and the devil didn't have anything to say. Then Chris and I laughed. But then we heard Sarah upstairs and we panicked. I shut the Bible shut. The paper crinkled and wrinkled. Then I slid the Bible on the bottom shelf and she came down the stairs.

A month later I'd already forgotten about it. I don't know why, but I'd just put the burned Bible back on the bottom shelf instead of throwing it away. Sarah and I were downstairs with one of Sarah's friends. I was working at my desk and Sarah was showing her friend the new floor we put down in the basement.

"O it looks nice."

"Yeah it looks really nice."

They were saying this type of shit. So Sarah's friend looked at the shiny floor and then she looked at all of my books on the shelves and she said, "So many books." Sarah shook her head and said, "Yep, he likes books."

Then Sarah's friend saw something on the bookshelves that interested her.

I heard Sarah's friend say, "O god, we used to have a Bible just like that when I was a kid. I used to love those big plush Bibles." I flipped around and watched the woman pull the burned Bible off the shelf and hold it. Sarah told the woman that she got the Bible a couple of years before as a wedding present. Then Sarah's friend opened up the Bible and the burned pages crackled and crinkled and popped up into the air.

Sarah's friend said, "Oh God."

Sarah said, "What the hell?"

I was caught. Sarah took the Bible from her friend and then Sarah was quiet. I didn't say anything.

I tried to think up what I should say. When I was in the 6th grade my friends and I stayed up late and drank a whole bottle of cheap wine my parents kept in the back of one of the cabinets. After we were done, instead of throwing the bottle away I just put the empty bottle back in the cabinet. The next summer my mother was cleaning and she came across the empty bottle I had put back in the cabinet.

She said, "What happened to this bottle of wine, Scott?"

I said, "It must have evaporated."

She believed me.

When Sarah asked if I knew what happened to the Bible, I didn't know what to do. I wondered if I should lie like I did when I was in the sixth grade and say I didn't know what she was talking about and give her a look like she was fucking weird. But I told her the truth. I told her Chris and I had burned the Bible. At first she just stood and looked at me like she was confused.

Then she said really quiet, "Why would you do that?"

Sarah's friend just stood and grinned a grin like she didn't know what to say.

But then Sarah started screaming, "Why would you do that? Why would you fucking do that?" Then she started shouting, "That's the Bible Mary Jo got me for a wedding gift."

And then Sarah's friend said, "I can't believe you would do that, Scott." And Sarah screamed some more at me and then she stormed up the stairs.

That night Sarah was still pissed and shouting, "Why would you do that?"

I tried to defend myself again. I told her it wasn't a big deal. It was funny. We didn't believe in any of this shit anyway, so what did it matter. I told her we were just bored.

Then Sarah said it just creeped her out. She wondered if there were more things I wasn't telling her about, people I was talking to. A different life I was leading. She told me you don't mess around with shit like that even if you are joking.

Then she told me she wanted it out of the house. She told me she didn't want the burned Bible in the house another minute. So I told her I'd put it in the trash in the morning but that wasn't good enough for her. She told me to get rid of it. I got up and went into the kitchen and got a garbage bag out. Then I swung the garbage bag open and it poofed out poof and full of air. I went downstairs and put the Bible inside of it. Little specks of the burned Bible fell off slow like snowflakes falling. Then I pulled the garbage bag string and tied it tight. "I'll put it out in the trash," I told her, but that wasn't good enough. She told me she didn't want the garbage men to see it. I yelled and told her that it was pretty fucking ridiculous to care what the fucking garbage guys would say.

But then I said, "Ok, Ok." I put my clothes back on and picked up my keys and I told her I'd get rid of it somehow. I left the house in darkness and I searched for a place to toss the Bible. I looked at the full moon and drove down the road.

I drove to the gas station and got out to throw it away but there was a guy with his back to me pumping gas in the stalls beside mine. I tried to push the big Bible in the trash can beside the gas pumps but the trash can was stuffed full of trash and so the big Bible wouldn't fit. I tried to put the big Bible in sideways but it still wouldn't fit. The guy who was pumping gas beside me still had his back turned towards me and didn't seem to notice. I heard laughing and it was the man beside me pumping his gas. He turned towards me and I saw his face and I saw his skin. He looked burned. The face was thick with scar tissue and the mouth looked melted and sculpted into a look of pain. So I just dropped the burned Bible down on the ground and the burned man just looked at me.

So I fled. I got in my car and I fled so fast away. I looked up at the full moon and I watched clouds slipping over and above it and below it all like knives. I saw the clouds make ghost shapes in the sky and I saw how silly it all was. And nothing happened.

It was done and I wasn't at a crossroads surrounded by an army of angels from hell. And I didn't see the future. I didn't see how my life was going to fall apart and how soon I'd be sick with swine flu. I didn't see how Chris' uncle would commit suicide two months after that and I didn't see how Chris would get divorced within the year. I didn't see how my daughter would be born so sick and small. And I didn't see how Sarah would say soon that it was over. And there wasn't the sound of ghosts haunting me. And there wasn't anyone showing me the future of my life and how everything I knew and loved would disappear soon. And there wasn't anyone there with a pitchfork and there wasn't the smell of sulfur. There wasn't the promise of a future apocalypse and the sound of things screaming or the weeping and gnashing of teeth. There wasn't a crossroads and there were no souls to sell. And there wasn't any such thing as Satan. There was only me. All Hell.

T he first time I met Sarah Johnson she told me I was going to shrink my penis.

She was wearing a black turtleneck and tights with a black skirt and black boots that came up to her knees. She looked like a cartoon character and she had big-big, big-big, big brown eyes. Her nose was small and her mouth was tiny like a dot. The dot turned down in the corner like a frown, but fuck descriptions.

I drank my Mountain Dew and she said, "You know that has yellow 5 in it? It's been known to shrink penises."

I took a chug from a big bottle and said, "That's why I'm drinking it. Need to take a few inches off."

She laughed like this: Say, O my god. O my god. Then say it for a million times.

*　　*　　*

The first time I heard Sarah Johnson tell a story was a few minutes later. She was talking about one of her roommates and how the roommate was getting her bean tickled that night. So Sarah was going to stay out and give her roommate some privacy.

I said, "Her bean tickled? What's that mean?"

Sarah smiled, pointed down to her crotch, and waved her hands up and down like they were pistols from the Wild West and then she said, "You know? Get that bean tickled. Gotta love them beans."

Then she winked at me.

Then she asked me if I liked beans.

I said, "Yeah, I like beans."

Sarah said, "Who doesn't? God bless beans."

So the first time Sarah Johnson touched my hand was just a few minutes after. I was in a rolly chair and Sarah was in a rolly chair too except she was rolling back and forth from her desk to another desk. She reached and grabbed my hand and pulled me to her. We rolled in our chairs around the room.

I said, "What the hell are we doing?"

Sarah smiled and said, "I'm chair dancing and you're doing it with me."

She told me there was a play she wanted to see that night and we should go together. She wanted me to go with her and I said, "Ok."

*   *   *

The first time I went on a date with Sarah Johnson this happened. I was 19 years old and she was 24 and I realized I'd never been on a date before. Never. She came by my room and I had a cut off t-shirt on and my teeth were fucked up because I'd broken one of the front teeth in half. I had shaved my head in the sink that week.

I offered her an Old Milwaukee. I was running behind. She looked at me and said, "Well, it doesn't get any better than this." Then she looked at the dirty room. Books everywhere, empty cans, papers scattered all over. She asked me why I didn't clean my room. I told her that I get depressed sometimes and then we talked and made jokes about using tampons as Christmas tree ornaments. Sarah laughed and I laughed. I knew right then that I liked making her laugh more than I liked anything in the world.

I put on a shirt and a tie and we went to a play based on Mark Twain's *Eve's Diary*. In the first act, we watched as Adam and Eve were cast out of the garden. In the second act, we watched Eve and Adam grow old. We watched Eve lose one of her sons. This was called aging. She looked at her face in the reflection of rivers and Eve imagined how it used to be. She worried about growing old. Adam told her that all flesh was a liar and we're just human now and in the end flesh fools us all. When Eve died we watched the actor who played Adam cry and when Adam buried Eve at the very end he said, "I used to think it was our great sadness having to leave the garden from so long ago, but now I see that I was wrong. Because you can only love what you lose. For I can see now that I never missed the garden from where we were banished. I can see now that wherever she was, there was my Eden."

Sarah turned to me and I rolled my eyes. I put my finger down my throat like I was going to gag and Sarah shook her head at me and smiled. We left before the play was over and went and talked.

Sarah told me later that night it had been a hard couple of years. Two years before she was driving home on the interstate and she had to pull over because she thought she was dying. She thought she was having a heart attack and the paramedics did too, but it was only a panic attack. They raced her to the hospital and left her car pulled beside the road and she was too afraid to do anything after the hospitalization because she was afraid she might die. So now she pretended she wasn't afraid but brave. She told me this was the story of the world—pretending. Then she asked me if I thought the play was stupid. Sarah said that if there was only one man and one woman in the beginning of time then we were all committing incest. The first generation of children would have to have sex with one another or with mothers and fathers to produce children. We laughed and she asked me if I liked the play. I told her it was corny and I told her I thought it was full of cliches. Then she laughed again and said, "Cliches. Just like our lives."

*   *   *

The first time I kissed Sarah Johnson was three days before Thanksgiving. I came over to her house and we watched a movie about a school bus full of children who died and then we watched a re-run of Jeopardy. I thought, "Movies about dead children are always good for romance."

I kept thinking if I should try it.

I kept thinking that.

I moved my head and kissed her on the cheek. Her face turned towards me and I kissed her on the mouth. It felt like:

zzzzzzzzzzzzzzzzzzzzzzzzzzzzzzzzzzzzzzzzzzzzzzzzzzzzzzzzzzzzzzzz
zzzzzzzzzzzzzzzzzzzzzzzzzzzzzzzzzzzzzzzzzzzzzzzzzzzzzzzzzzzzzzzz
zzzzzzzzzzzzzzzzzzzzzzzzzzzzzzzzzzzzzzzzzzzzzzzzzzzzzzzzzzzzzzzz
zzzzzzzzzzzzzzzzzzzzzzzzzzzzzzzzzzzzzzzzzzzzzzzzzzzzzzzzzzzzzzzz
zzzzzzzzzzzzzzzzzzzzzzzzzzzzzzzzzzzzzzzzzzzzzzzzzzzzzzzzzzzzzzzz
zzzzzzzzzzzzzzzzzzzzzzzzzzzzzzzzzzzzzzzzzzzzzzzzzzzzzzzzzzzzzzzz
zzzzzzzzzzzzzzzzzzzzzzzzzzzzzzzzzzzzzzzzzzzzzzzzzzzzzzzzzzzzzzzz
zzzzzzzzzzzzzzzzzzzzzzzzzzzzzzzzzzzzzzzzzzzzzzzzzzzzzzzzzzzzzzzz
zzzzzzzzzzzzzzzzzzzzzzzzzzzzzzzzzzzzzzzzzzzzzzzzzzzzzzzzzzzzzzzz
zzzzzzzzzzzzzzzzzzzzzzzzzzzzip.

We kept kissing and she said, "Why are you keeping your eyes open? It's weird."

I told her I was sorry. Then we kissed more, but I opened my eyes again. It was then that I felt like I was falling. Then I felt the cliches. I felt like I was falling with the cliches. I felt like I couldn't breathe and there were fingers choking me. Falling, suffocating. Everything was fine, as fine as ever, but then her stepbrother walked in.

Sarah said, "I thought he was gone."

Her stepbrother was embarrassed too. "O I'm sorry, Sarah."

Her stepbrother quickly walked up the stairs and Sarah and I sat up straight and Sarah told me she was sorry.

I told her, "I'm glad he didn't come in a few minutes later or he would have seen my little white ass bobbing up and down."

So Sarah told me to shut up and then she told me I was an idiot. She was right. So I shut up, idiot style.

But what did Sarah not know? I was 19 years old. I'd never kissed anybody. I drove home that evening and I thought, "Maybe I won't die because I've kissed someone now."

As I drove through the mountains, I wonder if I knew I would marry Sarah ten years later and we'd raise children together in the house I just left. I wonder if I knew that one day I'd be writing about how we met and how we only love what we lose. And how this chapter would end with a line from a play that two people saw so long ago. It would end like this, I wouldn't say I was sorry about what happened. For wherever she was—there was my Eden. In the memory we laughed and rolled our eyes and pretended we were gagging because it was all so corny and stupid. And it was all such a cliche. Just like our fucking lives.

B ut who was she? Her name was Sarah Johnson and she
was born in 1976 in West Virginia. She was the daughter
of Elphonza and Corrie. She had a brother named Jack who
I never liked but who I always said I liked. I never liked him
though and I'm not putting him in my book.

But if I really wanted to tell you about Sarah I would probably tell you about her first memory. Sarah was four years old
and she was taking a shower with her aunt Sherry. Sarah was so
short she only came up to Sherry's waist. They had come back
from swimming at the beach and Sarah had sand in her little
girl hair and sand in the folds of her little girl skin and sand
around the edges of her little girl bathing suit. And Sarah was
young enough to not be ashamed of taking a shower with her
aunt Sherry. Sherry slipped off Sarah's bathing suit and Sherry
took off her own bikini as well and the two of them stood naked

together beneath the falling water of the shower head. Sherry scrubbed Sarah down with a washcloth and then lathered up Sarah's hair and rinsed it free of sand. They switched places and Sarah stood and watched her aunt Sherry wash. Then Sarah saw something dangling between her aunt Sherry's legs. It was a white string. Sherry leaned her head back and rinsed her hair clean and Sarah felt only one impulse now. She wanted to pull the white string dangling from between her aunt's legs. She found herself repeating, "I want to pull the white string. I want to pull the white string."

So Sherry looked down and laughed at the little girl Sarah because Sarah had no idea that this was a tampon string. After the shower aunt Sherry told Sarah about the future and her aunt Sherry told her that some of us only bleed on the inside, but women are so alive that they can bleed on the outside too and make life. Like gods. So Sarah smiled and said she couldn't wait to be a god. But then one day she realized just how stupid this was and how her aunt Sherry was full of shit. This was a torture. And so after the shower Sarah went and sat with her father who she loved more than anything in the world.

His name was Elphonza. One morning, years later, he woke up after visiting Sarah. Sarah was a grown woman now and on the last day of his visit Elphonza started gathering up all of his stuff in the guest bedroom and was getting ready to leave. A few nights before he got up in the middle of the night and ate some tiny containers of ice cream Sarah kept in the freezer. The next morning, he told Sarah she needed to throw out the ice cream in the freezer because it had freezer burn. Sarah told him, "No it doesn't, Dad. You ate the ice cream I keep for the dogs. Frosty Paws." He didn't think about this now or how Sarah always laughed at him. He shaved and shat and packed his bags and finally showered after spending seven days with his daughter. Then he left. Later that afternoon Sarah went into the guest room to strip down the sheets off of her dad's bed and wash them. She pulled off the bed spread and the pillowcases and then tossed the pillow cases on the floor. Then she pulled down the rest of the sheets and something fell out. What the fuck? It was a giant chunk of cheddar cheese with denture marks around the edges.

So Sarah picked up her phone and called her dad.

"Dad, were you sleeping with a giant chunk of cheese in your bed last night?"

Elphonza said, "Hell yes. I was wondering where that chunk of cheese went."

When Sarah was a child, Elphonza sat in the evenings and drank his scotch and listened to Willie Nelson's version of "Always on my Mind."

The room filled with smoke and he watched TV some more. He watched car races and TV shows. He learned on a TV show about how there is no such thing as new water. He learned that the original water came from the Milky Way millions of years ago. It was carried on the back of a giant meteor and this giant meteor collided with earth and so life began.

And so we are all made of water then. We are all made up of what came here and collided and allowed something to be born and none of it is new. But he also learned if you wanted to buy the things that make up our bodies it would cost about as much as a candy bar. And that's all we are. Candy bars and stars.

Of course, Sarah knew if there was one thing Elphonza loved more than anything in the world it was Sarah's mother.

Her name was Corrie. One day Sarah and her mom went to go get pedicures and they were sitting in the pedicure chair and soaking their feet and then they put them on the pedicure footrest so the mani pedi woman could begin. The pedicure woman started rubbing the skin off the heels and the balls of the feet. Then the woman started working in between Corrie's toes.

The pedicure woman shrieked and stood up.

What the hell?

Sarah's mother had a tick in between her toes. And it wasn't just any tick. This wasn't a new tick that had been there for only fifteen minutes. This was a tick that had been there for days. It was the size of a giant ass shooter marble and packed fat and full of blood. It was pulsing and bulging and vibrating and growing and glowing fatter full of brightness and shining a rosy red.

"It's a tick," the pedicure woman shrieked and she walked away cursing.

Sarah's mom said, "O what's wrong?"

Sarah's mom looked down at her foot like she didn't even know what the pedicure woman was talking about.

Sarah felt like she was going to gag. "Mom, there's a tick between your toes."

Sarah's mom looked down at her foot again and inspected the chestnut sized tick between her toes.

Then she said, "Oh I guess I didn't notice it." This was Sarah's mother.

But then one day everything changed in Sarah's life. Sarah and her mother decided to do a production of *South Pacific* at a local community theater. *I'm going to wash that man right out of my hair.*

Sarah's mother was the lead in the musical and she never wanted to live in the mountains. She never wanted to be trapped and yet she didn't know that everything that winds up living in the mountains ends up getting trapped there. So Sarah watched her mother act in the musical and she listened to her mother sing in the musical and then one night she saw her mother see another man at rehearsals for the musical. She saw her mother's eyes shine alive again. They sparkled and shined, shined and sparkled. Then one day Sarah imagined the man from the musical was at Sarah's house and her father wasn't home. Don't tell your father.

Her mother and father got a divorce. Her mother moved out and her mother was gone. And Elphonza grew old. He was having heart problems and Sarah was afraid. She was ten years old and she thought her father was dying. So she snuck into his bedroom each night and sat at the foot of the bed and made sure he was still breathing. One night she listened to him breathe and snore and then breathe and snore some more but then Sarah fell asleep and forgot to watch him.

When she woke up a few hours later, she couldn't hear anything. She panicked. She hopped up off the floor and ran to the side of the bed and shook her father. "Please don't die, Dad. Please don't die." Her father woke up and said, "Sarah?" Then Sarah smiled because her father was still alive. Sarah smiled because he wasn't dead. He was just sleeping.

*   *   *

So Sarah grew up. She went shopping and she smoked pot and she went shopping and she hung out with her girlfriends. They were the type of girls who never worried about the world yet and who you would call this word: Gorgeous.

They went to parties and did mushrooms and fucked boys who had cars and boys who had jobs and they looked up into the sky together and talked about the boyfriends' beautiful cocks, big beautiful cocks, and Sarah reached up and picked the stars and put them in her pocket still high on mushrooms.

When Sarah was 16 she got a job working in the candy shop at the mall. One afternoon there was a little boy with his mother and they were walking towards Sarah's candy store counter. The mother of the boy was short and mom-fat and she did the talking for the boy who was skinny and had big teeth and glasses. Sarah watched as the boy stared at her.

He was carrying a bag from the bookstore and inside the bag a book that started, "Whether I shall turn out to be the hero of my own life, or whether that station will be held by anybody else, these pages must show." The little boy looked nervous and Sarah didn't know this yet but the little boy was always nervous. He thought about dying sometimes and he thought about going away. The mother of the boy asked him what he wanted. He whispered to his mother what he wanted.

He wanted candy raspberries and a medium blue raspberry slushie. The mother of the boy ordered them.

Candy raspberries.

Candy blackberries.

A medium blue raspberry slushie. So Sarah got the order for them and the mother paid and the boy and his mother walked away. And Sarah didn't think about it ever again. Nothing stood out. She forgot about it just like we forget everything in the world, but the little boy grew up and wrote this book.

S o twenty five years later we started to fight. We fought about this and we fought about that. We fought about this and we fought about that. We fought about this and we fought about that. And we fought about that and we fought about this. We fought about money and we fought about where we lived and we fought about how much I was travelling and we fought about how I was drinking and we fought about what I was doing.

We fought about all the tiny things. We fought about nothing and we fought about everything. It was glorious.

The worst fight we ever got into was the day when I came home and destroyed our computer. I walked through the door and I could tell Sarah was mad but she wouldn't tell me what she was mad about.

"Are you mad?"

"No."

"Why are you mad?"

"I'm not mad."

"You're being quiet and you have that totally pissed look on your face. Your mouth is all scrunched up like a butthole."

Sarah said, "Telling me that my mouth looks like a scrunched up butthole is probably not the best way to cheer me up." She told me to never use the word butthole in association with her face again. So I sat down on the couch next to her and tried to talk, but then I fucked up. I touched her shoulder and I touched her face and then I saw a little piece of fuzz on her chin. It was just hanging there. A little piece of fuzz, like a piece of dust, hanging there. So I reached over to pull it off. I put my fingers together to reach for it and then I pinched and pulled, except it wasn't a piece of fuzz.

It was a hair on Sarah's chin. Immediately her face formed into a face of fucking fury and Sarah started shouting, "What the fuck did you just do? What the fuck did you do?"

And then I started to say, "I'm sorry. I'm sorry. I'm sorry."

Sarah stood up and tears started forming around the corners of her eyes and she started shouting, "You know how sensitive I am about my face hair? Why would you do that? Why?"

I told her I thought it was a piece of fuzz. And then she settled down for a few minutes and then she shouted. She told me she was tired of fighting with me. She shouted at me that she was upset by what I'd been looking at on the computer. I asked her, "What was I looking at then?" And she had a look on her face like porn. Tons of porn. I told her she was exaggerating, but then she started reading a list off her phone. She'd sent it to herself in an email. She started telling me the names of sites like worldsex.com, youporn.com, mothersteachdaughters.com, bangbros.com, mycuckholdhusband.com, blacksonblondes.com, naughtyamerica.com, bigboobs.com, burningangel.com, mykidsbabysitter.com, youtorture.com.

Sarah looked at me and then she said, "Seriously, Scott? Youtorture.com."

Then she started listing off the names of the other porn sites. I told her, "Okay. Okay." I told her not to judge me about my tastes in porno. I told her when she read them all together like that she made me sound like a total pervert or something. Sarah just looked at me and rolled her eyes and said, "Well it's funny you should mention that because here's one called iama-pervert.com. And another called pervertcreep.com." Sarah said she wondered if I was talking to people online and I just shook my head and felt myself getting angry.

I shouted at her and she shouted at me. And then I shouted at her and she shouted at me and then we shouted together. And then we shouted in other rooms. I told her she was spying on me and she told me she knew everybody jerked off, but good god. We had kids now. I told her I was sick of her always complaining about every single thing I did. I started walking towards the computer room and I slammed the door to the basement behind me and I ran down the stairs. Sarah shouted, "What are you doing?"

And so I shouted, "Since I'm such a shit person I'm going to kill that computer."

Sarah said, "What?" and followed me.

I said, "I'm going to kill the computer" and then I started shouting, "Yep, I'm going to kill that computer" or variations like, "That fucking computer is going to get it" or direct threats to the computer like, "I'm going to kill you—you little fuck."

At the bottom of the stairs I went into the tool room and I grabbed a ten pound sledge that always sat in the corner. I picked up my sunglasses and put them on. Sarah said, "Why are you putting on your sunglasses?" I told Sarah that they weren't sunglasses anymore. They were safety goggles now. I told Sarah I was all about safety. Then Sarah said something about pictures, but I didn't know what she meant. I pulled at the computer but it didn't seem to budge. So I ripped at it some more but the wires were in such a rats nest of a tangled mess that I couldn't rip it right. We planned to get a new computer anyway because this computer had seen its better days. So I calmly pulled the cords out. 1,2,3,4. I took the monitor and I smacked it against the corner of the desk. I thought it was going to explode or shatter in glory but it didn't do shit. I slammed it a few more times and then I threw it against the side of the wall and watched it bounce and Sarah just stood there watching me. She had her hands on the side of her face. I reached down and grabbed hold of the hard drive and ripped it out of the wall and Sarah kept repeating, "What are you doing?"

I picked up the ten pound sledge and looked at her with a look like, "What the fuck does it look like I'm doing? I'm going to kill our computer."

I stood above the hard drive and swung the sledge hammer up like I was tossing a baby high into the air. The sledge came up heavy and I let it drop down dead. It smashed against the computer and bashed against the heavy plastic. Then I swung it up again and let it crash back down until the computer busted into about three or four separate computers and then I bashed those too. Then Sarah shrieked, "Scott. My pictures. My pictures of the kids." Finally, I knew exactly what she meant.

I killed the pictures of our kids and I looked down and there was blood all over my hand.

Sarah said, "Scott, I want you the fuck out of here and don't you ever come back."

She fell to her knees over the busted computer. And there was blood on my pants and there was blood on my hands and there was blood on my arms and there was blood on my pants and there was blood on my white t-shirt. I told her I was sorry and I told her I'd leave now. I told her maybe I didn't damage the hard drive. And now Sarah was crying. Since I was covered in blood, I decided it was a good idea to go out in public. Sarah looked back at me and said, "Scott, you're covered in blood." I told her I knew her training as a nurse was going to come in handy one day. But nobody smiled.

I went out to my car and I drove to the Super 8 motel and I got out. I thought, "I will stay here for the night." I tried wiping off the blood as best as I could and then I walked inside. The plain-looking woman behind the counter seemed nervous. She fumbled and bumbled with her computer. She looked at me and said, "Sir, I'm sorry but we're all booked up." I looked through the shiny glass behind the fake plant out into the parking lot and I said, "Two trucks and you're all booked up?" The one woman went and asked another woman and they whispered together like someone had died. They broke their huddle and then one woman came back and said they had a room.

She entered my info and told me I'd be in room 118. And so I repeated 118 even though it was written down on the folded paper that held the key. Then the woman behind the counter said without looking at me. "Sir, do you know you're covered in blood?" I didn't answer her. I just started walking down the red hallway from the lobby and repeating 118,118, 118. I repeated the numbers of the rooms on my way and said, 128,124,122. I counted them in my head like room 118 didn't exist at all.

I slid the card into the key holder and then the little light turned green. The lock unlocked in a buzz and then I pushed open the door and it was like I was pushing my way into my very own cell and I started crying. I called Sarah on the hotel phone and I told her how sorry I was and how sorry we should always be, always. I told her there was something wrong with me. And then I hung up the phone and I thought about the picture of us on the couch. I thought about the picture of us at the beach. I thought about us holding Iris in the front yard. I thought of Sarah sitting in a funny hat from years ago. These were moments of our lives.

The next morning Sarah called and told me to come home. She told me the pictures were all gone. But please come home. She was worried about me. And so it was. It was all gone.

I remembered the lines of an old book from my past and the lines were all different now: "Whether I shall turn out to be the villain of my own life... these pages must show."

What can I do? I can go back and place all the pictures I have left of my life and I can put them together. I can put them together in a book and so when Sarah is old she can take the book and she will be able to see them again and remember.

I'll put the pictures of Iris at the couch where she looks like a baby doll.

I'll put the pictures of baby Sam covered in kisses.

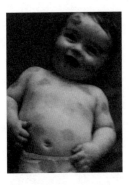

I'll put others too. And we'll all be here. In the pictures Sarah and her children will always be young. In the pictures they'll be young and alive. So she can return to them one day and we'll all be together again. Smiling.

It was around this time that Sarah told me she wanted a divorce. When she called me upstairs, I thought maybe she just wanted to have sex.

I came up the stairs and said, "Do you want to have sex?"

Sarah just shook her head and said, "No, I don't think we should, Scott. And besides, I'm not on birth control anymore."

So Sarah sat down on the loveseat and I handed her the baby who I'd just fed a bottle. He was sleeping now.

I told her, "O don't worry. We can if you want and besides Sam is sleeping."

Sarah told me she wasn't worried about getting pregnant. She told me, "I want a divorce."

I didn't know what to do.

I thought I heard her say, "I want a divorce, Scott."

Then I realized she said, "I want a divorce, Scott." She said, "I know you've been saying the past couple of times we fought that I've been trying to get out of this relationship for years." She sobbed. "But the truth is—I've actually been trying to stay in this marriage for years."

I sat on the couch and I watched her cry and I thought, "I wonder if she wants the divorce because of the nickname." A month or so before, Sarah had said, "I want a nickname. I've always wanted a nickname. A cute little nickname like Cee Cee or Sissy or something." I told her I had a nickname for her. Her nickname was the Moose. So I started calling her the Moose.

"That's not my name," she said. I said, "Whatever, Moose."

This went on for weeks and Sarah even started playing around with it. One day she left me a note that said, "*I'm going to the store with the kids. I'll be back soon. Love. The Moose.*"

I thought about asking whether the divorce was because I called her the Moose, but I didn't.

I decided to do something different. I decided to try and look pathetic. I tried out a disappointed and confused face and then I looked to see if that would change her mind. I looked at the floor and then I looked pathetic. I looked at the walls and I tried to look confused and full of fear. Then I looked at Sarah and she still wanted a divorce. I looked at my hands and then I looked pathetic. I put my head in my hands and I tried to look disappointed and pathetic and confused all at the same time. But then I looked at Sarah and she still looked like she wanted a divorce. I thought I should try something different.

I tried talking to her. I scooted over on the couch and sat next to her as she held Sam and he slept. Then I took my arm and I patted her on the back and she kept repeating, "You know it's not working. You know it's not." I patted her on the back like I was burping a baby and then I told her that she'd just had a baby not too long ago. I told her she'd gotten pregnant with another baby soon after the first.

I said, "That's two babies in three years." I told her she was probably just depressed. I told her that her hormones were out of whack and it was probably just post-partum.

Sarah's eyes popped open and angry.

Sarah rocked Sam and said, "How come when a woman is talking about how she feels some man has to go on about how her hormones are all out of whack or she's having postpartum. What the fuck do you know about postpartum, fat boy?"

Fat boy. So I scooted away and down the couch and I started to cry a kid's cry. I thought about chicken wings and how I wanted to fat girl the world. I told her I knew she didn't like the way I looked and lived. I leaned forward like I was bracing for the impact of an airplane crash and I started crying in one of these hyperventilating cries until I couldn't breathe. Sarah kept sitting in the chair and holding Sam and she said, "Settle down. Settle down. It's ok." But it wasn't ok. And so I cried and tried to catch my breath. Sarah said, "Settle down. It's ok." I cried and tried to catch my breath some more. And Sarah said settle down. Settle down. So I punched myself in the face like I did when I couldn't handle things and felt the sting against my cheek and then I did it again. Sarah shouted now, "Scott, please." And so I cried like a brat and said, "And you just sit there and don't try to comfort me."

Sarah just rolled her eyes and said, "Scott, I'm holding a baby." Then she called me by my nickname. Bubs. And Bubby. I whispered, "Excuses. Excuses." I felt wetness on my nose and wetness on the skin above my lip.

The wetness tickled a little. Then Sarah said, "Scott, you're getting snot on the couch." I was. I looked down and there was a snot smear on the back of my hand like a spider web in my hand hair. Then I saw the couch and there was a smear of snot on the couch cushion as well. Sarah tried to calm me and spoke in her mom voice now. "You know as much as I do that something is wrong."

I stood straight up and said, "Okay." Then I sat back down and said, "If you're not happy. You're not happy." I asked her if there was someone else and she said, "No." Then I told her if she wanted a divorce that I wanted her to agree to a few things. 1) "I don't want anyone else raising our kids" and then 2) I said, "Please don't move far away. Please." I started crying again and I asked her if she ever loved me. Her eyes dropped tears and she pointed to Sam and then she pointed towards Iris who was playing in the hallway. I stood up again and I told her I'd leave for the night. I picked up my keys and I held them in my hand and I let them dangle free. I walked towards the door but then I fell back on my knees in front of her on the floor and scooted towards her on my little knee feet. I put my hands together in prayer and I began to beg.

Please I said please.

No Sarah said no.

I told her I'd do better and I told her I'd stop drinking and I told her I'd take better care of myself and I'd cut out all the shit like eating chicken wings every night by myself and drinking and we could eat like a family again. I told her I'd go to therapy and I said please Sarah please Sarah please, but then Sarah said no.

Sarah said, "I've been trying to get you to go to therapy for years. I've been begging you to stop for years. And all the molestation stuff that happened when you were a kid."

So we stood and stared at one another and it was quiet and our faces were saying sad things.

I scooted away from her and then I stood up to say goodbye. I looked at her and I wanted to say something memorable and I wanted to speak the truest thing ever said between us. I wanted to say something that made her reconsider and remember who we were, but all I could think of was this, "You sure you don't want to have sex?"

Then I said, "You know, like a 'For the good times' thing. Like a 'One for the road' thing." She smiled and I smiled and she said she didn't think we should. I said, "Well would you at least think about it?" Sarah told me she'd think about it as long as I promised not to kill myself and I told her I wouldn't kill myself. Then we both smiled. This meant something. Sarah might have sex with me again if I promised not to kill myself.

I left the house that day and I drove to Walmart. I decided to sleep in my car that night and I decided to do all the things I couldn't do when Sarah was around. I walked inside Walmart and I bought a case of beer. I bought chicken wings from the deli. Then I took my bag of groceries and I went back and sat down in my car. I said, "This isn't too bad." I opened a can of beer and I drank it down. I felt the bitter bubble in my mouth and then I swallowed down the cold. I opened up another can of beer and then I drank it down too. I watched some porn on my phone and I masturbated. I wondered if the Walmart parking lot cameras could see me, but I didn't care. I didn't have anything to clean up with so I used a baby diaper I had in my front seat. I drank another beer and crushed the can and I threw it on the floorboard where it gathered with all of the others like little brothers. I made my little pile of a shiny can family.

I opened up the container of chicken wings and I pulled one out. I held the wing upside down all possum style and then I put it to my mouth. I ripped at the skin and garbled it down and I felt myself getting fat and I felt the whole world getting fat. I tore the meat from the chicken bone and I felt the chicken wing sauce sting on my lips and on the sides of my cheeks.

Then I talked to the chicken wings like they were still alive and I asked what the future held for me.

And the chicken wings just laughed and whispered a single word, "Pain."

I asked the chicken wings what the future held for all of us, what the future held for you.

The chicken wings just laughed and whispered, "Pain."

Then they laughed some more like maniacs and the chicken wings told me I was going to lose my mind starting now. I would want to die every day and there was a good chance that I wouldn't make it out alive. They said I was getting ready to live the worst part of my life. They said the planet Earth was dying anyway and they said the end had come and it was the Day of Judgment. Global warming and now the Day of Judgment was coming soon. They said human beings were over and done with and that the chicken wings were taking over. I just leaned back in my seat and smiled and said, "This sounds like a good time. This sounds like fun."

Sarah found out she was pregnant when she was 22 years old. She was dating this guy who lifted weights all of the time and they had broken up and then they got back together and that's when she got pregnant.

And now they were breaking up again.

Sarah decided to get it taken care of. That's what they said when they talked about it. "Get it taken care of." Sarah went out one night with her best friend, Hot Girl. She hadn't told Hot Girl about the pregnancy. So they talked about one of their other friends who had to have a breast reduction after years of back problems. Hot Girl told Sarah the latest gossip, "But now that she's had the breast reduction, she thinks they reduced them too much so she's going to get an augmentation. She's going to have to get big titties again."

They both laughed and they ate and talked some more and Sarah didn't say anything about what she was going through and Hot Girl didn't tell Sarah about her own heart. When they left, Hot Girl kept looking at Sarah and Sarah kept looking back. It was like Hot Girl was looking for something inside of Sarah, but Sarah didn't say anything. The next day the guy who got Sarah pregnant drove her all of the way to Charleston and Sarah was quiet and the guy was quiet too. They listened to songs on the radio.

Sarah thought about how when she was 15 she helped a church group picket an abortion clinic with Hot Girl and Sarah held up signs of dead babies even though she didn't want to.

When Hot Girl invited her, Sarah thought it would be a camping trip or something like that but she wound up holding picket signs of dead babies. Of course, Sarah didn't want to hurt Hot Girls feelings at the time. In the memory Sarah shouted louder and shook her sign harder. She was only fifteen years old. She was a good friend.

So Sarah thought about this in the clinic parking lot and laughed. She got out of the car and went inside the clinic. She stood inside the waiting room and a woman came to the window. Sarah signed in, filled out the paperwork and handed the woman a check.

The woman smiled and said, "Okay Sarah, why don't you come this way."

The woman was perky and she was saying all of these perky things. "Well, it's a pretty day outside isn't it? Oh gracious I hope it lasts."

The woman had Sarah sign some more papers and then she said, "I really like your purse."

Then the nurse gave Sarah a gown and Sarah put it on. The nurse examined Sarah and gave her an ultrasound. The jelly felt cold on Sarah's stomach and she shivered.

Of course, Sarah was nervous about her dad seeing her bank statement and wondering where the money had gone.

Then the nurse explained the procedure again. There would be:

1) An anesthesia.

2) Then an instrument would be inserted and the procedure would start.

Sarah laughed at this word "instrument." It made her think about her brother who played in the band. She thought about how her mother used to pop the pimples on her brother Jack's back and she thought about her own enjoyment at popping pimples. Pop. She saw far into the future when she would be known as the best pimple popper among the nurses at AHH Hospital.

"What is it that you like about it?" One of the nurses would ask Sarah.

Sarah would say, "It's like a pleasure thing. Like I just get satisfaction out of it. It's what I do. I pop pimples."

But now it was years before and Sarah was at the abortion clinic and she was still listening to the nurse's explanation about the procedure.

3) There would be bleeding and nausea afterwards and if Sarah noticed heavier bleeding when she got home or bleeding that was a darker red, then she needed to go to the emergency room.

Sarah rested on the table and the doctor came in and he was whistling.

What song?

Sarah couldn't tell.

The doctor asked her if she was comfortable.

Then the nurse said, "I was just telling her about how much I love her purse."

The doctor looked around and saw Sarah's clothes folded on a table and her purse on top of them.

He said, "O yes. It's a very nice purse."

Sarah thought. "Fuck yeah, purses!"

After the procedure was over they wheeled Sarah into a room where she could lie down and relax. It was full of cots and hospital beds and the beds full of a few women. There were hospital curtains around the beds. And there were women drinking orange juice and there were women taking care of other women. And there were women waiting for somebody to come and pick them up. And Sarah saw the women and thought it looked like a civil war battlefield full of bodies and Sarah saw there were wars waged on all of us. She sat down on a bed with a curtain around it and rested on her side. She tried to sleep but there was a woman on her side in the curtained room across from Sarah's. The woman had her back to Sarah and the woman was crying.

Sarah wished the woman would shut up. Sarah thought, "It's just an abortion. Good god. Book yourself a trip to the beach." But the woman kept crying. Then the woman finally turned over and Sarah could see who it was through the curtain. It looked like Hot Girl, but Sarah couldn't tell for sure.

The next time when Sarah saw Hot Girl, she didn't talk about it and Hot Girl didn't say anything either. Sarah didn't talk about summer days when they were girls and they used to play in the woods and Sarah didn't talk about how she used to be able to watch Hot Girl's house and she could even see Hot Girl climbing the fence when she came over to see Sarah. When they went on walks in the woods, Sarah always wanted to lead the walk. And they didn't talk about playing with Ouija boards and their boyfriends and how they were going to marry these boys or when Hot Girl went through a rebellious phase in the 8th grade and shaved her head or horoscopes or skipping school or when they got drunk and messed around together or leaving the door to their own houses unlocked. They left the doors unlocked so they could sneak back into each other's houses after the parents went to work and skip school. And then to sleep for a few hours together.

But Sarah didn't say anything about this when she saw Hot Girl. They were full of secrets now. They were like us. They were adults.

When the guy who got Sarah pregnant came to get her at the clinic he was smiling. He was with a buddy and they were drinking out of a giant plastic cup. They were drunk and they wanted something to eat.

They wanted to go to Burger King. So they left and went to Burger King and Sarah ordered chicken fingers and tried not to feel nauseous. She dipped the chicken finger in the chicken finger sauce and watched the sauce sticking to the chicken's breaded skin and she felt like a ghost watching herself and then she put it in her mouth and swallowed and it felt nice. The guy drove her all the way back to Beckley and no one said anything. So he dropped her off and no one said goodbye or I love you or I'm so sorry or what the fuck just happened or why is life so goddamn fucking weird?

Sarah thought about all the things that happened in this life that didn't make any sense.

Sarah turned to the guy before he drove away and said, "Thanks for the Burger King."

The guy said, "Yep, you're welcome. Burger King is good."

And then he was gone.

Sarah walked inside the house where she grew up.

And yes.

Burger King is good.

And sometimes she thought about it. Sarah knew it was silly but sometimes she used to hold something invisible and pretend that there were hundreds of lives apportioned to each of us.

In one life we are married.

In one life we are dead.

In one we are rich.

In one we are poor. In one we are parents. But always we belong to others.

I really wanted to kill myself, but I sucked at it. I had a bunch of Tylenol PM and some Pepto Bismol but I knew you couldn't kill yourself with Pepto Bismol. The next day after Sarah said she wanted a divorce I stopped by the house and picked up some stuff. I told her I was going to kill myself, but she didn't say anything. So I checked into another motel and looked through all the crap I'd picked up from our medicine cabinet. I opened up the first bottle of Tylenol PM and took out a handful of pills and then I drank them down. I started wondering why Sarah didn't say anything to me when I told her I was ending my life. Maybe she didn't hear me. I decided to call her up to let her know, but the call went immediately to her voicemail. I took another handful of pills and swallowed them down in a gulp.

Then I said, "I just wanted to let you know that I don't think I can take it anymore. I don't like it when you call me mangina sometimes. I'm an emotional man and you knew this when you married me. You're a great mother and a great wife but I don't know what went wrong. But just know I love you. Please tell the kids I love them too. Bye."

Then I poured out some more pills into my hand. I watched the pills wiggle out of the bottle as I shook them out. Then they rolled around in the palm of my hand like they were alive. I tried to swallow them but my mouth was too full of pills and beer and so I got choked and they came out in a gooey melty mess in my palm. I realized trying to kill yourself was hard and that's why people didn't do it more often. People didn't kill themselves more often because they're lazy.

I put the pills back in my mouth and then I drank them down and they were gone.

I thought, "What if something happened and Sarah never got my voicemail. Maybe I should leave another just in case."

I called her phone again and it went to voicemail and I left another voicemail. I said, "I just wanted to let you know that I can't take it anymore. You're a great mother and a wonderful wife. And I don't think you should call people names because it hurts their feelings. Please tell the children I love them. Bye."

Then I thought, "O shit. That's going to seem so weird if there are two messages that are the same."

So I called back and said, "I know it might be weird but I just wanted to make sure I left a message in case the first one didn't take. Okay. Bye."

I took the rest of the bottle and then I opened another. I popped the safety seal with my teeth and then I pulled out the cotton. "Fucking cotton," I said and then I poured some more pills into my palm. I took the first handful of pills and then I took the second handful of pills and then I took a third handful of pills. I realized something. Killing yourself with Tylenol was pathetic.

I'd always planned on hanging myself on the bar above my parents' garage door, but I knew that would hurt. I remembered a friend from high school whose girlfriend broke up with him and so he shot himself. It didn't work though because he just blew off the bottom of his face and his family found him and rushed him to the hospital. He lay in a coma for weeks but he survived. The only good part of the story was that his girlfriend felt sorry for him and so they got back together. They're still together now and a have a couple of kids. I thought maybe I should try shooting off part of my face instead. Maybe this would bring her back. I thought of the New River Gorge bridge and jumping. I sat on the floor of the Econo Lodge and I swallowed the rest of the second pill bottle. The pills were so bitter and bubbling up into my mouth and I burped and it tasted a pill taste on my tongue. Then I reached into my book bag where I'd dumped the medicine cabinet and then I stared at the third bottle I'd brought. It wasn't Tylenol PM even. It was something else. The third bottle I had to kill myself with was a bottle of children's Tylenol. I knew I couldn't kill myself with a bottle of children's Tylenol.

I decided to throw up. I went into the bathroom and I tried. I leaned over the top of the toilet. Then I put my finger down my throat and I gagged. I imagined people making fun of me. "How did he try to kill himself? He tried to kill himself with children's Tylenol and Pepto Bismol." I saw myself in a hospital bed surrounded by Sarah and her fellow nurses. They were all laughing at me and saying, "Mangina, mangina" and whispering what a fuck up I was. I jammed my fingers in my throat and then I gagged again but I couldn't throw up. So I took one finger and took two fingers and then three. I gagged until I felt the skin in the back of my throat. I felt the little thing that hangs down on the top of your throat and that nobody knows the name of and the warmth of air coming up from my stomach. I gagged gah. I tried to make sure I was throwing up quiet because Sarah always hated how loud I threw up. "It's like the most melodramatic vomiting I've ever heard. It's like someone who is making fun of someone vomiting." Then we laughed inside the memory. But then I realized Sarah wasn't here so I could throw up however loud I wanted. I stuck my finger deeper and then I gagged and vomited like who I was. I was the loudest vomiter in the world. Fuck yes. I was the champion of puke. So I puked up a clump of medicine. And it stopped. Then I did it again and all at once it started. I vomited up all of the memories and I vomited up all of the things that passed through my mind. I vomited up kisses and love. I vomited up the way she smelled like cigarettes and tropical fruit gum. I vomited up lists of the dumb things that we used to say when we were dating and made fun of one another over. I said, *I want to be as legendary as cheese* and she said, *Ok, I'm going to go piss our baby out.*

I vomited up the dumb jokes and the moments that were just moments and not stories.

I woke up the next morning to my cell phone ringing and Sarah scared in a voicemail. I texted her and she agreed to meet me later that day at the park where Iris and Sam were playing. When I got there, Sarah didn't really say anything except I scared the shit out of her. Then she told me I scared her pretty much all of the time now. Then she tried to change the subject and she started talking about work at the hospital. She told me that Rhani was mad because a patient looked at her and said, "That woman would sure look good behind a plow."

She told me she'd been having to digitally dis-impact this one patient who was bedridden. I asked her what that meant and she told me that it meant someone was constipated and their bowels were impacted with feces. Then she wiggled her finger around to show me how she digitally disimpacted asses. She said, "You have to get in there and pull out the feces with your finger." I shook my head and she smiled with joy. She said, "Seriously, you haven't felt true happiness until you digitally disimpact another human being." She told me most people die long deaths. Long deaths of shame. And she told me I should let her practice on me. I just shook my head no. I was depressed but I still didn't want her finger in my ass. Then she giggled crazy. She wiggled her finger around like she was digitally disimpacting me. It made me shiver. Sarah told me I should be happy I was alive and not dead. She pointed to Iris and Sam. I watched Iris and Sam playing in the rocks. I told her it was stupid what I did the night before and what an ass I was. I told her it was dumb anyway because you can't kill yourself by taking a couple of bottles of Tylenol.

Sarah didn't say anything for a little while and then she said, "Yes you can." She said people do it all of the time. They take a bunch of Tylenol thinking they won't really die and to get attention, but then they go into liver failure. She said they go into liver failure and a liver failure death was the longest and most painful death imaginable. She said "Who knows maybe if you hadn't decided to throw up you would have got what you wanted." Then she said, "Besides people kill themselves every day in acceptable ways." So I thought of people buying TVs and killing themselves. I thought about people buying houses and killing themselves. I thought about people working jobs they hate and killing themselves. I thought of people writing books and killing themselves. So Sarah put her hand on my shoulder and then she got up. She gave me a look like "Hang in there," and I was full of self-pity about my self-pity. I watched Sarah gather up the kids and put them in the car. Then she buckled them in their car seats and I watched them drive away. I saw into the future and I saw myself buying TVs and killing myself. I saw myself buying a house and killing myself. I saw myself working a job I hated and all of the tiny suicides of life. I knew there were a million ways to kill myself and I couldn't wait to try them all. [1]

---

1 I'm sure there is a Buddhist somewhere who is saying, All pain comes from wanting things and believing you possess things, but we truly own nothing in this life.

And I say to this Buddhist: FUCK YOU, BUDDHIST.

Seven years passed after Sarah and I watched the play. But then one day I decided to go to the mall. I was working as a teacher and I decided to go to a restaurant in the mall and eat lunch. In the seven years since I last saw Sarah, I'd searched for her number. She emailed me one time, but I accidentally deleted her email without writing back. Then time passed and I went to the mall one day and I had a cheeseburger and a diet coke and then I ordered a beer. I drank my beer and then I wondered whether I should go back to work or not, but then I decided to do something else. I decided to go to the bookstore at the end of the mall. I paid for my food and I walked to the bookstore. And then I saw this woman coming out of a store and it was Sarah. She was carrying a bag from the store and then she saw me. I waved at her and I smiled and she smiled back at me. I walked over to her and she held out her hand like she wanted me to shake it. Then we both laughed and I gave her a hug. I told her I was working in Beckley now and she said we should get together soon. So I asked for her number and she gave it to me. 3048275412. So I wonder who she would be if I called that number tonight. Would she be the Sarah from long ago?

And so this is a boring story about how I went to the mall one day and ordered a cheeseburger and my life changed because I ordered a cheeseburger. I didn't know it then but the story of our lives is the story of ordering cheeseburgers.

A week later I called Sarah and we went on a date except Sarah said it wasn't a date. She said we were just friends and that we were going to eat breakfast and then go back to her house and take a walk in the woods. Then she repeated. "Do you understand? This is not a date."

I was kind of happy it wasn't a date because my last date ended so badly. It ended with me in a mad dash running to a gas station bathroom after eating a ton of spicy food that didn't agree with me. "Well, did you make it?" Sarah said after asking me what my last date had been like.

I just smiled and shook my head, "No."

Sarah laughed and told me that this was the worst date she'd ever heard of and why was I honest with her. She told me shitting your pants is probably not the best way to get a second date with anybody. Then she just shook her head and started filling up her plate with breakfast food from the restaurant buffet.

I filled up my plate too. And then we sat down and talked about our lives. We talked about her schooling and my job. She told me about her last boyfriend and then she kept making fun of me about the gas station bathroom incident. She said, "You just tell me now if you need to go to the restroom. I don't want any accidents this morning." And then she ate some more and we talked. We talked about some of the movies we'd seen and then we talked about her family. She asked me what I'd been reading recently and I told her about this Buddhist monk who spent years writing a letter about what he knew about love and the human heart. I'd been reading how the monk studied and meditated for years and never let anyone inside his shrine where he always worked on his letter. After he died the other monks opened the letter up and it was blank. He'd written nothing. We both laughed at what a shitty monk the guy was. Then we talked about other things. Sarah told me funny stories about her dog and then she played me a funny voicemail from her dad.

Sarah told me she'd recently heard on the radio that more people get divorced today because they're living longer. That's the only reason why. People are just living longer. If your husband's dead at 28 you don't have to worry about divorcing him at 40. Then we laughed at how wise we sounded and ate some more.

I finished up my plate and stopped, but Sarah ate eggs and then she ate sausage links and then she ate two pancakes and then she ate a fruit salad.

So eggs.

Sausage links.

Pancakes.

Syrup.

More eggs.

Fruit salad.

Then Sarah kept going back to my embarrassing dating story. She said dating was ridiculous and we fell in love just because the world told us to. It's expected of us and maybe it was better to be alone so you don't shit your pants in front of someone. I told her that maybe love was just chemicals released in our brains to make us pass on our genetic make-up. But then Sarah went back for another plate. We laughed about what a great eater she was and she ate a bowl of grits and a bowl of cereal and then more sausage.

A bowl of grits.

A bowl of cereal.

Sausage.

After she was done Sarah stretched her arms out and accidentally hit the woman sitting in the booth behind us with her hand. The woman turned around and Sarah apologized. I made a motion with my hand to the lady like Sarah had been drinking. We all laughed some more and then Sarah acted like she was still hungry.

She said, "I might get one of those cinnamon raisin buns."
And then she ate that too.

We paid and we took off to drive back to her house where we could walk through the woods and hang out and talk. We drove and talked and she talked about how people become different people when they are with different people and the person we're with is just a collection of the people who came before. She told me that she thought we are only a collection of other people's ideas about us. We are all a we. I told her we sounded like a bunch of stoners and then I told her about my teaching and how hard things had been the past couple of years.

Then Sarah grew quiet. I was talking and she was listening, but she wasn't saying anything back.

It was like she was whispering inside, "I don't need a bathroom. I don't need a bathroom."

Then she took her hand and touched her stomach and she whispered, "O god."

Just a few minutes later I heard her burp a soft burp. It's the type of burp you think no one can hear but they always do. Then the voice she heard inside her head suddenly changed.

It was saying she needed a bathroom now.

So she gripped the door of the car and I drove along. Then Sarah calmly said, "Scott, I think I'm going to need to find a bathroom soon." Then she giggled and told me she was sorry for making fun of me about my last date and this was her punishment.

I drove, I drove and asked, "Do you need me to pull over?"

She told me we were on the interstate. She couldn't just stop in the middle of nowhere beside the interstate and squat. So I hit the gas and zipped down the mountain road with a mountain on one side and on the other side of the road a cliff.

Holy shit, a cliff.

I told her it's fine. Don't worry.

Then she snapped and said, "Will you please stop talking, Andrew?"

I thought "Andrew?" Andrew was the name of the ex-boyfriend she told me about.

I didn't know what to say but then Sarah said, "I know I just accidentally called you by the name of my ex-boyfriend but can I please apologize later?"

I stopped thinking about it and I kept driving. I didn't think pretty people even used the bathroom. I thought about the Buddhist priest who spent his whole life writing one letter on what he knew about the human heart. He would leave it for those after his death and it would say nothing. I thought about monks and love.

So I pushed the gas and drove down Sandstone Mountain.

I started pulling in and out of the tractor trailers and through the smoke that was coming off their brakes. There wasn't a gas station around.

I heard Sarah breathe deep and I whispered, "Hold on. Hold on."

There was the exit.

So I zipped and dodged and whipped around trucks whispering, "Hold on. You're going to make it."

And then Sarah said, "I don't know."

And then there was a fucking coal truck and then cows crossing.

Hurry up, coal truck. Hurry up, logging truck. Hurry up, you fucking bunch of cows.

And then there was more speed and the gravel road and then there was the dirt road and then the house and a bathroom. I stopped in front of her house.

Then she said, "Ok, ok, ok, ok, ok."

She popped open the car door and she took off running and I watched her run.

I just sat and watched her and I wondered if she was going to make it. I said, "I think she's going to make it." But I stopped talking and I just watched her run. I knew one thing for sure. None of us ever make it in the end.

PART TWO

I told Sarah I was going to live at Walmart until she changed her mind about the divorce. After I lived there a week, I decided that she wasn't going to change her mind. So each day I sat and watched the buggy boys gather up the buggies and take them inside. I watched the people with handicapped stickers pull all the way up and park in front. I decided to call Sarah and check up on the kids.

I told her, "Well if you need me, you'll know where to find me." Then I shouted, "O god!"

Sarah said, "What's wrong?"

I told her, "O don't worry. I think I just saw the biggest woman I've ever seen going into Walmart. I wish you could see her. Hold on. I'll try to take a picture."

But Sarah said, "Yeah, Barbara said she saw you in the Walmart parking lot. She asked me why you were there. It's embarrassing people seeing you there, Scott." She told me she needed to give me something and I knew what she meant. She wanted to give me some money for an apartment.

I told her I wasn't going to take any of her blood money and she told me I would. I told her I wouldn't and she told me I would. I told her no. This is where I live now. She told me no you don't. Then I tried reciting a love poem for her but she told me I was drunk.

"I don't need her goddamn blood money," I repeated after we hung up. "She's not even romantic. Won't even let me recite poems to her?"

Then I sat in my car and looked out at the parking lot and said, "These are my people. This is West Virginia." And they were. I watched the customers walking from their cars and into the store and when they came back to their cars their buggies were full of stuff. One buggy. Two buggies. Three buggies. Four.

They were shopping for groceries to take home and make their children grow. I sat in the car and drank my gin from a water bottle. Then when my bladder got full I went inside and peed. A white car pulled up at the end of the parking lot and just sat there. I decided to call the guy driving "Big Pimpin'" and when Big Pimpin' parked it was always the same. He was a skinny looking little white dude who had dread locks. He sat in the white car and then a few minutes later another car pulled up. A redneck looking dude got out and walked over to the white car. I wondered if they ever tried reciting love poems to someone.

I watched the redneck dude lean inside the window. It looked like they were exchanging something and then the redneck dude got back in his car and drove away. Then Big Pimpin' drove away. I waved at Big Pimpin' but he didn't wave back. It was okay. These were my people. But then just a few minutes later Big Pimpin' pulled back up again. There was a girl inside the car with him now and she had dyed looking blonde hair and a skeleton face. They waited together and then a blue beat up van pulled up. The meth looking girl got out of the car. She was inside the van for about a half hour and then she got out and went back inside Big Pimpin's car. She was trying to put her shoe back on. I sat and thought up my own review of Walmart I could post online. I watched them drive away and I wrote inside my head.

I highly recommend the Walmart parking lot for living in your car after a divorce. The cops don't seem to bother you if you park close to the entrance. I did notice quite a bit of drug related activity at all hours of the day. There is obviously some prostitution going on in the parking lot as well. Yay life. 4 stars.

That night I watched people leaving and the lights glowed from the parking lot. I went inside and used the bathroom. I looked at CDs for about a half hour and then I came back out and moved my car to the other side of the parking lot so the cops wouldn't give me hell. I noticed a text from Sarah that said, "We need to talk about getting you some money so you can get an apartment."

I wrote back, "I'm not taking anything. And how come you won't let me recite love poems to you? Seriously."

She never texted back. So I leaned my chair all of the way back and I put my jacket over my head and I slept. I dreamed about people going inside and buying all of the things that made up their lives. I dreamed about the whole world becoming just one big parking lot and we were all living there thinking about what we could buy. The next day I woke up and someone was knocking on the window. It was Sarah and she was wanting to give me some money for an apartment. I unlocked the car doors and she walked around to the passenger side. There were people going inside the store again and there were some kids playing.

Sarah sat down in the passenger seat and said, "We have to talk. You have to get out of here and let me give you some money."

I rubbed the sleep out of my eyes and Sarah said, "Where do you go to the bathroom?" I pointed to the empty Gatorade bottle on the floor. And then I told her I went inside to use the bathroom a lot too. I snuck my toothbrush in each morning and brushed my teeth in the sink. I said, "And then when I get bored I go in and play the video games they have set up in the electronics section. It really helps to pass the time."

I told her that I loved going inside after midnight and watching all of the people of the world shop. They were the people who the rest of the world didn't want and they were the ones who didn't belong anymore. They were the people with amputated arms and they were the people in wheelchairs and they were the people with face tattoos and scars. I was a scar too. I was a giant human scar. And then I felt serious and I said, "Walmart is more than a store. Walmart is a state of mind."

We laughed and I started to rant.

I told her people always bitch about Walmart putting mom and pops out of business and killing the small businesses of our country. But who did the Mom and Pops put out of business? Who did they fuck over? They fucked over the blacksmiths, but you don't hear the blacksmiths bitching. I told her I was on the side of the blacksmiths.

Then I told her about my dreams. I told her the whole world was going to be like this one day and the world was just going to be one giant parking lot and people would live to shop at Walmart and buy stuff. I was quiet for a second. "It's going to happen. The people will come. And they will bow before it all." Sarah finally had enough and she wasn't letting me talk anymore.

She was watching a woman emptying out her buggy and said, "You would think that woman has enough beef jerky." She looked at me and said, "Scott, I want to give you something. I don't want you living here anymore."

I was going to change the subject again or try reciting poems for her, but then I told her my life wasn't just money to get an apartment. I told her I hoped I meant more than a little bit of money to make someone feel better. I told her I'd stay here for the rest of my life if I had to and I didn't believe in the stories the world tells us to make people feel better about themselves. Then I told her I didn't have enough money to get an apartment anyway.

Sarah said, "Well I have a way to fix that for you. I have a check for you." She reached into her purse and pulled it out. She told me it was from part of our savings at the credit union and I told her she wasn't going to buy my ass off so easy. I wasn't just someone you could give money to and they'd shut the fuck up. Sarah tried to hand me the check but I wouldn't take it. She told me it was 4,000 dollars and then she threw it on my lap. The check said, 4,000 dollars. So I did what life teaches you to do when someone wants to give you money. I shut the fuck up and I took it. I took it because my life was worth 4,000 dollars.

Finally, Sarah got out of the car without saying goodbye. I didn't say thank you and she didn't say you're welcome and Sarah went and sat down in her car and then she drove away.

As she was driving away I felt the need to say something to her. I wanted to say how much she meant to me, how much fun we'd had and how that's what no one ever talks about or can explain—the fun. And the fights too. We had the best fights and where did it go? Instead I just looked at the check and thought, "Sarah has such nice handwriting. Another reason I love her."

I went to the bank and I deposited the check. Instead of going somewhere else I came back and sat in the Walmart parking lot and I watched the people go inside.

I watched them fill up the buggies and forget about all of their pain. I knew that all of the people would be coming soon and so I decided to join them and become one of them for a moment. I got out of my car and walked towards Walmart. It glowed in front of me like a temple. I walked and walked and then I saw Big Pimpin'. He sat for a few moments and then another car pulled up beside him. I watched him park and then I waved at him. This time instead of ignoring me like he usually did, Big Pimpin' raised his hand up and then he nodded at me and said hello and we were friends now. So I went inside and saw the aisles rise like castles before me. And there was beef jerky, and almonds and chicken wings, pizza bites and cheese, all kinds of cheese, steak, pork chops, crackers and cereal. There was Fruity Pebbles and potato skins and soda, Mountain Lightning soda. And there was Red Bull, diet Red Bull, beer, light beer, dark beer, pistachios, juice boxes for kids, air mattresses to sleep on instead of beds. And there were CDs and there were DVDs, saline solution for my contacts, potato chips and dip for potato chips. I had 4,000 to spend and there were things here to keep me alive. And so I walked among the aisles. I thought about Sarah and her telling me to be quiet when I recited my poems and I thought, "What kind of damn person doesn't like poems?" I could see outside in the parking lot and the people were coming for a coronation of some sort. And so I walked among them because these were my people and this was my kingdom. They would all be bowing soon. This was the new country we had made from the skeleton of the old one. And I was their king of beef jerky. I was their emperor of soda.

I finally found an apartment though. My name was Scott McClanahan and I wasn't a fucking alcoholic. My name was Scott McClanahan and I had an apartment. On the day I moved all of my shit out of Sarah's house I kept telling myself, "No matter what happens today—just remember that you're going to celebrate. No matter what happens today just remember that you're going to drink a bunch of beer tonight." So I walked all the way to the U-Haul place to pick up the truck. The cars and trucks whipped by me on the road as I walked and I watched my step and wondered if I should fall in the path of the trucks. I walked on the back road and there wasn't even a sidewalk. If you would have seen me that day you would have said that's the loneliest man in the world and it's hard to believe but he had a mother once. It's hard to believe but he had a father once too.

I picked up the U-Haul and drove to the house where I always parked and got out. There was a little boy who lived next door and who always used to talk to me and his name was Eddie. He came over and said, "Hey Mr. Scott. My Mom said you're getting a divorce."

I wanted to tell him, "Hey Eddie, your Mom told me you were adopted," but I didn't because I think he already knew he was adopted and had only come to live here a year or two before. That's the problem with adopted kids who know they're adopted. You can't hold some secret surprise over their heads. I told Eddie it was true about the divorce and I told him I wouldn't be seeing much of him anymore and Eddie said that was too bad.

I walked down the front yard and behind the house. I knew Sarah had left the basement door to our house unlocked and all the boxes were inside. I thought, "That's when you can tell when somebody wants a divorce—when they pack up your shit before you even get there." I opened the basement door and said to myself, "No matter what happens today you can drink beer at a restaurant and it'll be okay. You can drink beer at a restaurant and you'll still feel like a living human."

I picked up the first box and moved it into the truck. Then I took another box and moved it in the truck. I was sweating now like I always sweated because I was the greatest sweater in the world. Eddie told me that I sure did have a lot of books and I told Eddie that was true and then I told him that was the best thing about reading. You can always be somebody else. You can see the whole world from a ghost. Time travel and all that shit.

I moved a box and I moved another box. I did this for hours. The sweat popped and rolled down my skin and stained the boxes all wet. On one of my trips outside, Eddie asked me if I was sad and I told him I was trying not to think about it. I told him about my plan to drink that evening at a restaurant and feel alive. Eddie followed me and told me he didn't think I should do that. He told me he didn't drink because he was only six and then he told me he read the Bible. I wondered if Eddie's mother was happy that she didn't have to see me peeing out the back door anymore. I wanted to tell him that she caught me one night, but peeing out the back door was a god given right for every human being, and this is what god intended.

Of course, I don't know what made me do it but I decided to go upstairs and leave Eddie behind. The day before, Sarah had asked me to stay downstairs when I moved my stuff out. She had taken the kids to her mother's and I promised her I would stay away the day before, but for some reason I felt myself being drawn upstairs. I told myself, "Whatever you see up there just know you're going to be okay and in a few hours you'll still be alive." I shot up the stairs and opened the basement door like always. I walked around and saw it all and there were pictures of Iris dressed up like a biker with a bicep tattoo. There were pictures of me holding Sam. There was the Buddha light switch which stuck out below the Buddha belly like a penis. I flipped the Buddha penis on and my steps echoed in the upstairs and the rooms seemed so empty and alone. I thought, "Why do houses seem so small that way? Is it because we are leaving them? Or is it because we have left them long ago?"

I walked to the kitchen and opened up the fridge. Then I saw something on the table like Sarah was working on a project or something. It looked like she was putting something in a giant frame. I went over to the frame and turned it over and there it was. It was a diploma for a Dr. Jones. I knew he was a doctor she worked with at the hospital. What the fuck was his diploma doing in our house? So I called Sarah up and said, "What the fuck? You already have your boyfriend's shit in the house before I even move out." Sarah said, "First off, he's not my boyfriend and you know this. Second, I thought you promised me that you weren't going to go up the stairs. I knew you'd act crazy."

I asked her, "Well, if someone asks you not to come up the stairs what the fuck are you going to do?"

We shouted for fifteen minutes. Then I tried to recite a poem for her, but we started fighting again. She told me she was just doing something nice for someone and I told her I didn't give a shit. Being nice was overrated. I was going to drink beer that evening. I said Eddie told me he was sad to see me go and then I told her that Eddie likes me and gets me. He always did. Sarah said, "That's because he's six years old, Scott."

I asked Sarah if she gave a shit about what she was doing to people like Eddie. Sarah said he'd get over it. We shouted for another fifteen minutes until I slammed the house phone down and went back to the basement.

I moved some more boxes and then Eddie came back and said, "Are you okay Mr. Scott? I heard you shouting upstairs a few minutes ago." I told him I didn't know if I was ever going to be okay again and I didn't know if any of us ever would. I told him I wished this for the rest of the world.

I moved the last box of books and slid it in the back of the truck. Then I came back and looked at the basement. I looked at the dead plant outside that I always peed on behind the back porch. It was always dead and Sarah never knew why. I walked around the basement and it was so empty. And everything was gone. And then in the corner I saw the dust. I saw some of the dog's hair and then I saw one of Sarah's hair scrunchies she always used to put her hair up in a ponytail with. I thought about Sarah and I thought about pony tails and I felt like I was going to cry. I whispered, "Sarah."

I told Eddie he wouldn't be seeing me anymore. I asked him to look over Iris and Sam when they played in the front yard and I asked him to help look out for our dog Bertie when she ran away. Eddie said, "Don't be sad, Mr. Scott." Then he said, "At least you can go to the restaurant now." I shook my head "Yes" because Eddie was right. Even though he read the Bible he was absolutely goddamn right.

I drove the moving truck towards the restaurant so I could order beer and be the king of my underworld. The truck bounced and shook and I decided on the way there to get a steak. I passed the fast food restaurant and the fast food restaurant signs were sticking up like monuments. I saw the fat people and the skinny people and the big people and the little people go inside and I felt like one of them. I wanted to call Sarah again and recite a poem for her. She told me she never could understand what I was saying anyway because my accent was so thick. So I drove beside the people, but we weren't afraid. I saw the fast food signs stretch in front of me and I knew that if I met a person from the future who returned to here I would say this is who we are and this is what we were.

I drove on and the steering wheel felt like I was driving a truck made of air. I could have stopped at the fast food places except they didn't serve beer. So I drove to Applebee's and parked the moving truck and went inside past the pictures of people they had in every restaurant. I felt like I was different and I felt like I was more alive because I could enjoy this. I knew how wonderful the world was and I knew there was someone somewhere who would be eating the same steak I ate and drinking the same beer I drank and it was this that made us one. "Welcome to Applebees," the hostess said in the same uniform that someone else was wearing somewhere else. And I saw her wearing clothes that someone else had made and make-up that someone else was wearing somewhere too. A woman named Michelle handed me a menu and she had a name like the name of a million different Michelles but she was her own Michelle. When she asked what I wanted to drink I said I'd have a beer. Then she smiled and said, "Of course." She said, "May I see your ID?" I smiled and said, "Thank you for asking" and I opened up my wallet. I was sweating from the moving and my face felt like it was slimy and shining a greasy shine. I looked for my license and it wasn't there. I looked in between the cards in my wallet and it wasn't there. I felt inside my pockets and felt nothing. Then I remembered I took it out when I went to the bank. I told her I didn't have my ID and she said she was sorry. She told me she was being watched because the state was cracking down and someone lost their job just last week serving alcohol to a minor.

And then she told me that I looked so young and I told her it was the devil's confusion. He let me look good as long as I felt bad. And so I should have begged and told her about my day but I didn't. Instead, I tried not to cry. I ordered a salad and a steak and a diet coke. I finished the diet coke. And when they brought me the food, I ordered another diet coke. Then I ordered another one after that. And then I drank that one and ordered another. I thought about how there were things in the soda that were slowly killing me and I drank it down and said, "Delicious." Then I finished the steak and I thought about all the dead animals I killed and I said, "Delicious." I ate my salad and I knew that even the tomatoes felt pain, and we just didn't know how yet. I heard the carrots crunch and cry and plead for their lives and I said, "Your death tastes delicious, carrots." I told the salad it could only grow because of the bones of the dead and the skin of rot. And so I said, "You taste delicious too."

And so I killed everything I could kill and it felt like fun. Then I paid for the dinner and I left.

When I got back to the apartment I didn't even start unpacking the boxes. I just simply parked the moving truck and went inside. I walked to the kitchen and reached beneath the sink where I put the bottle. I pulled out a gallon sized jug of gin and then I went upstairs and sat down on my air mattress and I drank. I drank from the bottle and then I drank from the Gatorade. I thought, "Remember to stay hydrated." The sun was setting behind the apartment and I looked out over the lot and the locust trees and parking lot stuff. I could see the back of the stores and I knew I was different because I could say it looked beautiful. I could mean it too.

I drank some more and then the bottle began to disappear and I sat in my bed and passed out and then I woke up and drank some more. I drank until everything was fuzzy and fun. And then the whole room got drunk. I fell asleep and I felt something between my legs and on the sheets beneath me. I looked down at the bed and there was a circle of wetness and the wetness was brown. It was shaped like a halo. I touched it and then I realized it was shit. I'd shit the bed. I felt the wetness on my butt and smelled my shit stench. My name was Scott McClanahan and I'd just shit the bed. I wasn't what people said I was. I was Scott McClanahan and I was celebrating life.

After Sarah and I moved in together and fell in love, I used to do this thing I called the day of debauchery. I woke up one morning and thought, "I feel like having a day of debauchery today." I picked up my wallet and all of my wadded up dollars and sticky nickels and then I drove to the store and I bought a case of beer. I bought a couple of bags of potato chips and I bought cheese. When I got back, Sarah asked me what I was doing. I made a little trumpet sound with my mouth bumpety bump bah bah and announced, "Today is an official day of debauchery." I asked Sarah if she felt like doing it with me.

Sarah said, "No."

I said, "O come on. Why don't you?"

But Sarah kept watching murder shows on TV. They were usually about husbands or wives who snapped, but this one was about serial killers. Sarah said, "I'd totally let Richard Ramirez murder me." Then we saw them talking about Richard Speck and how later in prison Speck grew female breasts with the help of hormones. He grew them in order to survive. "Man, Richard Speck has some nice titties," Sarah said. And he did.

They looked like this:

I wondered if this was the same impulse. To kill and love: to possess and consume and destroy something like a child.

So I two fisted some beer. But then I started getting upset because Sarah wasn't doing the day of debauchery with me.

"O come on. Please?" I asked, but Sarah just kept watching her TV show. So I went into the bathroom and shut the door behind me. I jerked off and then I had an idea.

I wanted beef jerky. Bad. I walked out the door and she asked me where I was going. I told her I was walking to the store to get some beef jerky. I thought, "She doesn't understand my love of beef jerky. She doesn't even know me." Sarah laughed and kept flipping back and forth between a History Channel documentary and the serial killer shows on the TV.

"It's 9:30 in the morning, Scott," she said. "I know it's the day of debauchery but I don't want you complaining about how you ate too much beef jerky later."

So I tried to open the front door of the house, but it wouldn't open. Fucking door. It finally opened and I was on the porch except there was a broken brick on the porch that always fell off if you stepped on it wrong. So I hopped the broken brick which no one ever fixed. "Fucking brick, " I said and I walked up the yard and around the hole where we had a big ass stump removed a month or so before.

I walked around the edge of the hole but I kept looking in the hole. Then I felt myself losing my balance and then I was falling. FUCK. I was falling in the hole. Stupid fucking hole. I stood up and tried to look cool but there was nothing to cover it up. I'd fallen in a hole.

Sarah opened the door and said, "Did you just fall in a hole?"

I picked the leaves off my poofy sweater and I tried to wipe the mud off the knees of my pants.

I said, "No." And then I started drunk crying.

Sarah said, "Well, why are you crying?" I walked back to the house and I told her it was true. I'd fallen in a hole and I'd lied about it. I kept crying. Sarah asked what she could do.

I said, "You could do the day of debauchery with me."

Sarah smiled.

A few minutes later I passed out in the back bedroom, but when I woke up I smelled pizza. Sarah had just gotten back from the store. She had two pizzas and a whole order of chicken wings. And there were cheesy breadsticks and there was beef jerky. There were two cartons of ice cream and some cookie dough and she was eating the cookie dough. She was eating the ice cream too and watching the television shows about murder. Then she went back to the kitchen and got a couple of pieces of pizza and some breadsticks and some wings. She ate the pizza and then she ate the wings and then she ate the bread sticks. Then she drank a big glass of milk and then she drank another big glass of milk and then she went to the bathroom. I didn't know what was going on. She told me she wanted to be the best day of debauchery buddy in the world and then she shut the door behind her. The water was running and then she was in the bathroom for a little while and then I heard the toilet flushing. Sarah came back and her eyes were watering. I didn't know what was going on, but I sort of did.

She started eating the ice cream. She didn't even put it in a bowl but just started spooning it out of the containers and eating it up. She ate big bites and the ice cream dribbled down her chin. She ate the whole thing of ice cream and then she went back to the kitchen and got another slice of pizza. Then she ate that too. She went to the bathroom and turned the water on. Then I heard flushing and she came back and I asked her if she was okay. She just smiled and asked if binging and purging was an acceptable day of debauchery activity.

And so I knew what I should have done.

I should have said no.

I knew I should have said this wasn't okay and she had taken it too far. But instead I just smiled. Instead I said inside my head, "I accept you. I accept you forever."

And by accepting her, I said this, "Will you accept me?"

So we sat together and accepted one another.

She started telling me about her eating and I told her about my pain. She told me she'd been doing it since she was a girl. She told me that the only thing she feared was the dentist because the dentist always knew. Dentists knew everything. Then she told me about all of the horrible things. She told me there were horrible things like a college boy who took her to the liquor store when she was 13 years old. He was so heavy and she couldn't get out of the front seat. She saw him a few years later in her brother's yearbook from college and the guy was smiling. She told me about her secrets and I told her about my secrets too. We shared our secrets together.

She ran into the kitchen and picked up a knife. She started laughing and said we should kill ourselves together. I couldn't tell if she was joking or not and so I started eating too. I ate pizza and I ate cookie dough. And then we started making plans. We talked about what murders we would make, and we talked about what banks we would rob. I felt my belly fill full and then I went to the bathroom and I was purging. I put my hand down my throat and I tried to breathe. I felt myself gagging and then the vomit baby that lived inside my belly started to push its way into my mouth. Then it was gone and I listened to the toilet water trickle and splash. I felt my stomach grow empty and rumbling and ready to be filled full again. I pushed the toilet handle and I watched the throw up islands disappear down the toilet in a cyclone surge of water. I wiped my mouth from throwing up the whole world and when I came back we talked about hijacking planes and we laughed. We talked about our revolution and the toppling of governments and the History Channel docs they would make about us one day. And we would do it together. We talked about the assassination of presidents and we smiled. We would start our revolution together and execute our enemies. We talked about taking over the world and how there would only be us. And so I shouted it now, "There is only us, Sarah. There is only fucking us."

I t was around this time that Sarah got a job working as a nurse in the ICU. She used to come home in the evenings and tell me about working at the hospital. She told me about a young man with cancer whose bowels were impacted and how he was probably going to die. She told me that he'd developed an Anorectal Fistula.

I said, "What the fuck's that?"

Sarah told me that's where the body essentially creates a new asshole for you. The acid burns right through the skin and leaks shit.

I said, "The body can make a new asshole for you?"

Sarah told me that the body can do anything. So I imagined my body making new assholes. I imagined myself covered in assholes.

Sarah told me about another guy who was in need of a fecal transplant. She told me about his wife and how she cried and looked afraid.

I said, "What? Wait. A fecal transplant?"

She told me about how when the body has been through so much chemo it no longer reacts to antibiotics. Therefore, the doctors will transplant feces back into the body of a patient. There is bacteria in feces that will fight against infection.

I said, "Does it have to be your own personal feces, or will it come from like a feces donor? If so, does the feces donor have to be related to you?"

Sarah told me to shut up.

I asked, "What about accepting feces from another species? Would monkey feces have the same impact?"

Sarah told me to shut up.

The next night she told me about the schizophrenic. He was 6 foot 5 and there were tattoos on his neck and tattoos on his eyelids and there were tattoos on the top of his shaved head. There was a note on the door that the nurses in psych made for him, "*Please be careful around me. I suffer from delusional thoughts and hear voices that tell me to hurt friendly people like you. Please don't help me hurt you."*

Sarah heard about how he'd broken a nurse's nose the week before. He thought she was the devil and he was god. Sarah wondered why everyone thought they were either a god or the devil. Sarah wondered, "Why doesn't anyone hallucinate about how they work at a grocery store?"

So Sarah sat down and washed his feet and started communicating with him. She noticed he had a devil's face tattooed on his forearm and a nurse from the psych ward came in and told Sarah to make sure she kept her back to the door. Sarah said, "Don't worry. I won't let him get out." The psych nurse just laughed and said, "No, honey. We're not worried about him escaping. We're just worried about him getting you stuck in the corner and beating you to death." Then Sarah took care of the schizophrenic and looked at the tattoos on his arms.

She said, "O that's so pretty. You have so many of them on your arms too."

The schizophrenic guy looked at her like "Ah fuck. Here I am in the middle of a complete psychotic break with fucking Susie Sunshine."

So Sarah kept looking at his tattoos and there was one with a star and a date inside the star.

"Is that your birthday?" Sarah asked.

The schizophrenic guy didn't answer. Sarah thought about his birthday and tried remembering what his sign was.

She said, "Are you a Pisces? No."

"Are you a Sagittarius? No."

"Are you a Libra? No."

The guy finally had enough. He said, "I'm a fucking schizophrenic."

They didn't know what the hell the other was talking about. We never do.

That afternoon the psych nurse told Sarah about the nightmares inside of the schizophrenic guy's mind. There were devils and death and righteousness and rot and feces and a hand exploding. But then the next day he was still talking to the voices inside his head and they gave him medicine.

He wasn't getting any better though.

So they zonked him out and he wasn't getting any better.

Sarah had an idea. Sarah looked at where his devil woman hallucination always sat and said, "Can you believe she just said that?" The schizophrenic guy looked at Sarah like someone finally understood.

He said, "Yeah she's always running her mouth like that. You can't get her to stop. You just have to ignore her skank ass."

Sarah had another idea. She walked over to where the hallucination was standing or at least where the schizophrenic guy was looking and Sarah took her finger and pointed at the devil woman and shouted, "You know what? I really think you need to shut your big ass mouth, bitch."

The schizophrenic guy looked like someone was finally making sense. Someone was finally helping. And Sarah acted like the devil woman was trying to start some shit.

She said, "What did she say?"

The schizophrenic guy said, "I hate to tell you this nurse but she called you a 'cunt' a few minutes ago."

Sarah said, "She called me a what?"

So Sarah started wrestling with the air. She punched a punch and she kicked a kick and she started putting the air into a headlock before she finally kicked another kick until the devil woman ran out of the door in a zoom.

Sarah shouted after her, "I don't ever want to see your tramp ass again or I'm gonna rip out those fake ass hair extensions. You trashy bitch."

Then Sarah smacked her hands together and said, "Shoo wee."

The schizophrenic guy said, "Thank god she's gone. Finally."

Sarah smiled and knew the world was just one big hospital and we were all trapped inside of it. Then she thought about the invisible things. She thought about gravity and she thought about wind and she thought about the most invisible thing of all.

D ay after day it was like this. We had our days of debauchery and lived our lives and Sarah came home and told me
about how crazy her fellow nurses were. She told me how she
caught one of them screaming at an 80 year old man. "Didn't
your mother ever teach you how to clean your fucking foreskin?
You must have had a horrible mother."

She told me about what nurses spend their money on.

Titties. Fake Titties. She told me about how one of the
nurses used a credit card to pay for a breast augmentation and
then defaulted on her credit card. Sarah asked the nurse if she
was nervous about not paying back the money for her operation.

The ER nurse just pushed out her chest and wiggled her
tits around and said, "I'm not worried. They don't repossess
titties, girl."

Then Sarah told me about the old man who was her favorite patient.

He was this patient who had diabetes and who'd just had his leg amputated. Sarah told him he looked like a pirate now since he only had one leg. The old man didn't hear her at first but then he smiled and said, "Argg matey." The old man didn't have any family though and he didn't have anyone come visit him ever. The old man was almost deaf or at least all of the nurses thought he was almost deaf until one night Sarah noticed that his ears were dirty.

"Gracious, it looks like you need your ears cleaned," Sarah said and took out her tweezers. She pulled out the clot of wax and looked at it. The wax was the size of a baby finger.

"I bet that feels better," Sarah said.

All of a sudden the old man shouted, "I can hear. It's a miracle. I can hear." But it wasn't a miracle. It was just ear wax.

Then one night Sarah told me a story about death. It was three o'clock in the morning when they brought this young man back to the ICU and he was already brain dead really, but they were keeping him alive. They were keeping him alive so his mother could drive from North Carolina and say goodbye. Sarah took report from the ER nurse who told her, "Gunshot wounds to the chest and the spine and throat. It had happened a few hours earlier. A family disagreement." There was also another shot that was lodged in his skull. Sarah looked at the young man and touched his arm and listened to the ER nurse finish report. She told Sarah that the patient had come from North Carolina for the weekend to protect his sister from an abusive boyfriend. Her brother brought his pistol and there was a confrontation with the abusive boyfriend. Shots were fired and here he was.

Sarah imagined about what his day had been like. She imagined how earlier that day he had been playing video games with his nephew. She imagined how earlier that day he'd been throwing the football. He kissed his sister's cheek and touched her pregnant stomach and then that night he was shot and now here he was and he was dying. So Sarah called the dying man's mother on her cell phone and updated his status. The mother had Sarah put the phone to her son's ear. She told her son to stay alive. She told her son she loved him in case she didn't make it there in time and then Sarah hung up the phone and she checked his vitals again. It beeped in the background and then it beeped again. She went and hung another IV. She saw the tattoos on his knuckles and the teardrop on his cheek. She saw the claw on the side of his neck. Then Sarah thought of the worst tattoos she'd ever seen.

There was the one where she took off this kid's pants one night and he had two tattoos. There was one on each knee. On the right knee it said, "Fuck" and on the left knee it said, "You."

So Sarah smiled and thought about another tattoo she saw on a guy who overdosed. It was on his bicep and it said, "Mother. The only lips of another man's wife I've ever kissed."

Sarah straightened up the sheet on the man who had been shot. It rested and twisted beneath all of the tubes. Then she looked down and saw a tattoo that ran the length between his hips and above his pubic hair. It ran straight across him and just below his stomach. Sarah wondered, "What did it say?"

Sarah pulled the gown and the sheet away for a moment and she looked at it. It said, *The Bedroom Bandit*. Sarah laughed and then she whispered to her friend Rhani who was standing outside in the hallway and filling out a chart. "Hey Rhani, come here." Then she wiggled her little finger come here and Rhani finally walked into the room. She asked Sarah, "What?" and Sarah lifted the sheet and pointed out the tattoo. *The Bedroom Bandit*. Rhani laughed too and then she looked close.

"What is that beneath it?" Rhani asked and then they both looked closer. There were two small pistols beneath the words *The Bedroom Bandit*. And the two small pistols were smoking and beneath the two small pistols were tattoos of something else.

"What is it?" Sarah said.

Rhani smiled and said, "Pussies."

So Sarah looked closer and it was true. It was two tattooed pussies and the pussies were smoking too. But then they both heard something outside in the hallway. Rhani left the room and went back to work and then Sarah turned around and another nurse said, "His mother is here."

Sarah quickly covered back up the bedroom bandit's tattoo. She knew this wasn't something he ever expected his mother to see. The mother came in like she was in a trance.

She walked over to her son and she whispered, "My baby. My baby."

She stopped crying and she thanked the bandit for being her son and she thanked god for allowing her to be his mother. She told him he was a good son. She told him she would see him again one day in heaven.

Sarah reached down and tried to make sure the sheet stayed put around the bedroom bandit tattoos. But then the mother moved her arm from around her son and the sheet slipped.

"Oh, I'm sorry," Sarah said and tried to pull the sheet back up so the mother couldn't see the tattoo. But then the mother saw it all and stopped Sarah.

The mother said, "What's this on my son?"

The mother looked at the tattoo and didn't say anything. she took her fingers and ran them over the length of the tattoo. The B. The E. The D.

Sarah said, "I guess sometimes we do things and we don't think our mothers will ever see them." His mother didn't say anything. She told Sarah, "No, I'm glad he liked life. I'm glad. And it looked like life liked him back." Then the mother told Sarah that he was a good son and she wanted Sarah to know that. Sarah smiled too and his mother was still smiling a soft smile an hour later when they removed her son from life support. The mother held his hand and kissed his swollen face. And then she told him to go home. To go home. He never belonged to her anyway.

Then Sarah thought of all the true tattoos we never get. She wondered why people didn't tattoo themselves with the truth like *I am not a butterfly. I am not a unicorn. I am not a snake. I'm afraid. I'm dead inside.*

But these are the tattoos we wear inside our skin. These are the tattoos placed on the tissue of our hearts and they all say the same thing, we are all losing the things we love.

I thought Sarah had a boyfriend maybe. Even though I'd already moved out and we were getting ready to sign the separation papers, I was still coming over to the house and watching the kids when she was gone. So one afternoon after she left for work I went into the back bedroom and went through her stuff. I opened up the tiny drawers of her jewelry box and looked through them for some kind of proof. I opened drawers full of her clothes and shut drawers full of her clothes thinking I'd find the love letters from someone new. I opened and shut drawers and listened to the children cry from their high chairs in the kitchen. I shouted, "It's okay babies. Just hold on. Daddy's trying to find proof that mommy is cheating." The kids didn't care and kept screaming like I was just a paranoid asshole. So I went back to looking. I picked up an old yellow purse she'd been using earlier in the week and I went through it. I found some wadded up chewing gum wrappers and an old empty pill bottle from the weight loss clinic.

I threw the old diet pill bottle back in the purse and I heard the children shouting some more so I said, "Settle down children, your mother is on drugs. She's on speed." I put the purse back in the closet. Then I went through some dirty clothes she had in the corner and I emptied out her pants pockets and I found more lists. There were lists that said, "Gray Goose vodka and tattoos." Tattoos? Then I found a wadded up white post it note and on the white post it note was someone's handwriting and a phone number 304-979-5450. I took the white post it note and walked into the kitchen and quieted the kids down. I handed Iris some grapes and I gave Sam a set of plastic keys to keep him occupied. I didn't tell them that I found the phone number of their mom's new boyfriend and how the man on the other end was the one breaking up our family.

They just played and giggled and ate. I picked up the phone in the kitchen and tried to dial the number with shaky hands. The phone rang and I tried thinking about what I was going to shout at him or if she was with him now. The phone immediately went to voicemail. And then I heard the bastard's voice. "You've reached *Scott McClanahan of Beckley College.* Leave a message and I'll get back to you." Fuck. The children stared at me like I was a dumbass.

I said, "Don't look at me like that. It's an honest mistake. How many times have I ever called myself at work?"

So I decided to chill the fuck out. I told them that this still didn't explain the receipt for the department store that said *men's wear* from a month ago. I fed them and I cleaned them and then I sat them in front of the TV. I went to where we kept the new computer and I logged on to the department store's website. I looked at the product number on the receipt. 7aj665. In the other corner of the receipt it said: quantity. 3. I imagined dress shirts and ties. I imagined sports jackets and new pants. I imagined new clothes she'd bought for a new boyfriend. I tried to type the item number in the search bar of the department store website but nothing came up. I pulled down to men's wear on the web page and watched the department page pop up. I scrolled through the department page searching through the item numbers. There was 7aj658, 7aj675, 7aj621. I couldn't find it. That evening before I put the kids to bed I was packing some of the clothes I left behind and I realized there was a bag from a department store over in the corner. Inside the bag were three packages of underwear that Sarah had bought a month before. The men's wear was mine.

I decided to stop acting crazy. A week or so later I talked to her on the phone when I was at work and Sarah said her mom was coming over to watch the kids because Sarah needed to say goodbye to her friend Kimmy. Kimmy was leaving the hospital for another job. I knew Sarah had worked with Kimmy for years. I said, "Well, tell your boyfriend I said hi." Sarah asked me how I was doing with the paranoia and I told her I felt like I was doing better. We laughed some more and then we hung up and I went back to work and then just a few minutes later the old thoughts started creeping in. I thought, "She has someone else and that's the reason for the divorce." I thought, "She has a boyfriend and is making up that Kimmy story. She's going to go see him I bet."

I left my office and got in my car. I drove down the mountain and got caught at the red light. I said, "Come on. Come on." I waited and I wondered what was wrong with me. I thought about long ago when she loved me and I thought about how she walked barefoot in the shadows of our floor. I thought about the sounds we made. I thought about how I went and got us hamburgers from Wendy's on that first night we were together and we ate them in the kitchen with the lights off. I thought about how the sound of poems felt inside my mouth. But now the red light turned green and I drove. I felt my heartbeat and I thought about Dr. Jones and I remembered years before when we saw him at the mall and Sarah's eyes were shining. And I thought at the time that she'd never looked like that at me. He was a lung surgeon who moved into the area. Lungs: Where we breathe and live.

I thought, "I'm not going to the hospital because she probably isn't saying goodbye to Kimmy at the hospital. I bet she'll be at Dr. Jones' office." I pulled into the clinic of where Dr. Jones' office was and I passed the cars in the parking lot looking for Sarah's. I saw a Ford mini van. I saw a Dodge mini van. I saw a bunch of beat up cars with plastic in the window spaces and I saw a bunch of doctor cars and I saw a Toyota. I saw another Dodge mini van and I saw a black Honda CRV. I stopped my car and got out and then I looked inside. There were two children car seats inside. There was the car seat of Iris and there was the car seat of Sam. The children were with her mother. I thought, "Motherfucker. I've caught you. You're not going to see Kimmy. You're going to see Jones."

So I walked into the office complex and decided to just stand behind the door of Jones' office. I wanted to see who might come out. I sat and waited. The door opened once.

It wasn't Sarah.

The door opened twice.

It wasn't Sarah.

The door opened three times. No Sarah.

But then the door opened again and there was Sarah walking out of Dr. Jones' office. She looked skinny and stepped with a quick step to her car.

I walked past her and said, "How's Jones doing?"

Sarah looked confused. "Scott? What? I was seeing Kimmy."

I saw anger flash across her face. She shouted, "Goddamnit, Scott," and then she started shouting and yelling and telling me she was sick of my shit. She told me I needed to see a psychiatrist. I started apologizing. "I'm sorry. I'm sorry." She said, "I told you I was going to say goodbye to Kimmy. It's her last day. It's this type of shit that made me ask for the divorce in the first place."

I told her I thought Kimmy worked at the hospital with her, not in Jones' office and then Sarah told me I was an idiot. She told me Kimmy worked in Jones' office. Then she repeated. "I'm fucking sick of this. I'm so fucking sick of it." Then she slammed the door to the car and shouted at me from the open window of the car. "Kimmy hasn't worked in the ICU for years. She's been working in this office since she left the ICU."

So imagine me mouthing the words, "I'm sorry." And imagine Sarah pulling away.

I drove out of the doctor's parking lot and I told myself to stop being crazy again. I took some deep breaths but then I started thinking about the bad things. I thought, "I bet she's lying though. I bet Kimmy doesn't work there." I drove all the way back to my office and I thought up a plan. I'll look up Dr. Jones' office number and see if Kimmy really works there. I sat at my desk and looked up the number on my computer. I looked through the people who worked in the office on the website and I didn't see anybody named Kimmy. I saw a Margaret and I saw a Samantha but no Kimmy. I figured that this Kimmy didn't even exist. My hands were shaking so bad I dialed the wrong number. I started again and dialed the number to the doctor's office and then the phone rang. And then I waited.

A voice answered. "Hello, this is Dr. Jones' office."

I asked the man, "Yes sir, is Kimmy there?"

I knew Sarah was busted.

The man voice said, "Yes, this is she. This is Kimmy."

I didn't know what to say.

It was Kimmy. And she wasn't a man. Her name was Kimmy and she was a woman. Her name was Kimmy and she existed. So I told her I was sorry and then I hung up. I knew I was wrong about everything and I hoped I'd never be right about anything ever again.

The next day Sarah called me and said we needed to sign papers. We didn't get lawyers though. We just met at the courthouse lobby and we didn't say anything to one another. Sarah's face was all puffy and she had tissues in her hands and she kept wiping her nose and crying. Her hands shook when she handed me the papers and she cried some more and I touched her hand. Then she signed. Then she signed again. Then she signed some more. Then I signed. Then I signed again. And then I signed some more. I told her I didn't want this and I wanted her to change her mind. Sarah told me she would make copies and file them with the court. Then she gave me the second set of papers we signed. So this was the beginning of the end. We just had to take a child parenting class now and the divorce date would be set. It was all so easy. And it was all so fucking boring. Just like our lives.

Later that night I sat and read Ovid and the first line that says, "I shall speak of how everything changes." I saw that there was something else I knew about the world besides losing things. And it's this. No matter what happens, everything changes. I thought, "Are you happy right now? Well just wait."

T he day after we signed the papers my air conditioner froze up. My mother was helping me clean and it was hot as shit and we turned the AC down too low. I called the air conditioner repair guy to come check it. I kept looking out the window for him and telling my mom how happy I was to be in the apartment and not hanging out in the Walmart parking lot with a bunch of drug addicts. There was a mosque in front of my apartment and I liked to watch the families arrive on Fridays. I told her it was a tender mercy in my life and it was better than the weirdos from the parking lot. My mom told me it was getting so bad in Rainelle that the pill heads were breaking into the houses of old women to beat them up and steal their pills. She said an old man died in town and somebody robbed his house while the family was at the funeral. I just shook my head and told her I was glad that dad had the home security system put in. Then I showed her the air mattress that I'd been sleeping on.

I said, "I mean who'd ever need a bed when they have a kick ass air mattress like this?" I thought I heard the repair guy outside but no one was there. I kept looking out the window through a little hole the previous tenant had cut in the blinds to see if anyone was coming to arrest them. My mom asked if it was a queen sized. I turned back to the air mattress and looked at my mom like "Hell yes, it's a queen sized." Then I said, "I'm not some cheap ass. This is the Cadillac of air mattresses."

We both laughed and she said, "Oh Scott. What's that?" Then she pointed down at the end of the air mattress where I'd taped it.

I said "What?" and she pointed again.

I said, "Oh that's where I had to tape it because it has a hole in it." Then I told her I had to fill it back up each morning because the air leaked out during the night. When I woke up in the morning I was always sleeping on the floor.

My Mom said, "And you're going to have the kids sleep on this?" I told her not to worry about it. I told her it was just a metaphor for life and that it would all be okay. I told her it would be a great adventure. I told her I wasn't having to live in the Walmart parking lot anymore and having to deal with all that crap. I told her I liked watching the families coming to the mosque on Fridays and it made me feel nice. So I nodded my head and Mom put her hands on her hips and said, "Okay" and then she gathered up all of her stuff and kissed me and told me she loved me. She told me it was going to be okay and she told me that when we're at our lowest we're not. It's when we're at the lowest that we're actually in the arms of god. She told me that god shows us love through our suffering. That suffering is a hug from god, but we just can't see. I didn't tell her that she was ridiculous. I just told her not to worry and it was all going to work out and then I told her that Sarah would change her mind soon. I promised. I looked out the window and said, "Hopefully the repair guy will be here before too long." Then I watched her walk out the door and get in her car. I waved at her from the window and she waved back at me.

A few minutes later I heard somebody else pull up. I heard a door open and then I heard a door shut. I figured it was finally the air conditioner repair guy. I went to the bedroom so I could change the old sweaty t-shirt I was wearing and put on a new shitty t-shirt that wasn't sweaty. Then I took off my old pair of jeans with the holes in them and put on my new jeans which only had a hole in the knee. I went back to the window and I looked outside. But it still wasn't the air conditioner guy. It was a really nice car and there were people outside and there was a woman in the front seat. And in the driver's seat was a young guy who looked all muscular. In the back seat was another guy, but I couldn't really see him. I thought, "What nice looking people. They must be coming to visit someone in the apartment building."

I pulled away from the window, but before I did I saw something out of the corner of my eye. The pretty girl was holding a hypodermic needle and sliding it into a vial of something like you see in doctor's offices. Then she pulled out a rubber tourniquet. And it swung in her hands like a dead snake. I watched her wrap the tourniquet around and around the arm of the guy in the driver' seat. She went tap tap tap against his arm like she was trying to wake someone from sleep. And he just kept holding his arm out straight like a stick. I watched her poke with the needle and miss and then try again. I watched her put the needle down and I realized that they didn't know anybody in the apartment building. They were just getting high.

I watched the girl finish the guy up. His head fell back like his head was now a concrete head and he needed a place to put it. I watched the girl do the same thing to herself. She wrapped the rubber band around her stick arms and then she stretched and then she tapped and then she poked and then she shot and then she watched the rubber band go limp. I watched the guy in the back seat take it from her. Then she started looking at her arm and there was blood dripping down it. She licked her thumb against her tongue. Then she wiped the blood away until her arm was bare. But the blood was still smeared there. So she started to lick at her arm until it was all gone and then she dabbed at her arm and she couldn't see the blood anymore.

I turned away from the window and I went to the bedroom. I blew up my air mattress all the way. I watched it rise and fill full and become a bed. Then I decided to re-tape the electrical tape. I picked at the roll of tape with the tip of a finger until an edge of the tape came loose. And then I ripped it off with my teeth. I re-taped it and stretched the electrical tape thick and tight. I drew the blinds and I looked out the hole at the people in the car. They were still there and they were still high. I turned off all the lights and I walked to the air mattress. I sat on the air mattress and I knew there was only one lesson in life. Tonight I would start sleeping on air but by the morning I would be sleeping on the hard floor. I felt the air mattress beneath my butt and I heard the air escaping sssss and I felt all of the air in the world escaping from me, sss. I thought about all of the horrible things in the world.

I thought about Rainelle and all of the old women getting beat up for their pills and being left lonely with only black eyes and swollen skulls. I thought about the old man who died and who had his house broken into while the family was at the funeral. I thought about one of Sarah's patients who was in the hospital for days and wasn't getting any better and then finally Sarah found out why. The old woman had a bunch of fentanyl patches stuffed down her throat. I thought about all of the sad things in the world but then I thought about the families arriving at the mosque.

I stopped listening to the air escaping sss and trying to keep it from escaping behind the tape. I got up and I ran down the stairs. I wanted to say something to the people doing drugs in the parking lot. I wanted to shout something joyous at them. My feet made the stairs creak and then I put on my shoes at the front door. I made sure they were still outside. And they were. I laced up my boots and I walked out the back door and around the apartment building.

I left the door open and I noticed the air conditioner guy had pulled up and was getting his paperwork ready to come inside. But I didn't say anything. I just kept walking and then I saw them. And they saw me. All three of the people in the car stopped and they stared and they looked scared of me. The girl in the passenger seat slapped at the arm of the guy who was driving like, "Let's go. Let's get the fuck out of here. That guy looks insane." The guy driving gunned the car backwards and then he spun the tires and drove away. I watched them rip away and I chased after them and shouted. "Please take me with you. I'm so lonely here. I want to beat up old ladies and take their pills" I shouted at them just like I'm shouting now. "Will you be my friend? Will you?" Then I pretended I was an air mattress and said, "Sssssssssssssssssssssssssssssssssssssssssss." I watched them disappear in the distance and all I could do was say, "I accept you."

Four years earlier, Sarah and I got married, and then we got a dog. His name was Mr. King. He was this 18 year old pug who was blind as shit and who needed a home. "He looks fucking blind," I said when I came home one day and Sarah was holding him in her lap. "It looks like his eye is missing." I looked at the empty looking eye socket and it was all gooey and full of pus and empty from where the eye should have been. I told Sarah we shouldn't keep him, but she told me it was okay. "Yeah he got one eye ripped out a few years ago, but it'll be okay," she finally admitted. "We can still keep him though because Mr. King is a good boy."

Then she told me how he lost his eye. It happened years before over Thanksgiving when Mr. King was left alone with some other dogs. Mr. King was so good looking that the other dogs beat his ass because they were jealous and then ripped his eye out.

"Fuck," I said.

"He's a pretty boy," Sarah said and petted him some more and Mr. King opened his mouth and panted ugh. His teeth were all broken and missing. They were weird ass barracuda teeth on the top of his mouth and then he started scratching and I noticed his pink lipstick pop out and pulsate every time Sarah petted him. Sarah kept telling him, "Yes, Mr. King. You're a horny boy. You're just a big ole horny boy." I told Sarah we shouldn't keep him.

Sarah told me it was okay and then she told me he was just a little bit blind. But then she put him down on the ground. She told me that's what people like us are here for: To take care of the helpless things. So Mr. King cocked his head like he was listening for something. Then he took off running as fast as he could at full speed and slammed straight into the living room wall. "I don't think he's just a little bit blind," I said. Mr. King bounced off the wall like a battering ram and fell onto his side. He sat there for a moment and then he stood back up on his legs and cocked his head like he was listening for something again. We couldn't help but laugh. Then Sarah picked Mr. King back up and held him in her lap some more and petted him. I looked at his other eye and it was all blue and cloudy and it looked blind too. Then Sarah finally admitted Mr. King was *really* blind. She told me that the Thanksgiving after the dogs ripped his first eye out, the dogs jumped him again and this time they fucked him up and blinded his other eye. I told Sarah it was going to be a problem since we couldn't train the blindness out of him.

I petted him a little bit too but then I noticed this white looking ooze coming out from his penis. I backed away and told Sarah that there was something wrong with his dick too. Sarah looked down and said, "Yeah the vet said he has testicular cancer. That's the reason why he smells the way he does." Mr. King got down on the floor again and started scratching. He scratched around his neck and he scratched around his arms. Sarah just looked at me and said it would be alright.

But it wasn't. Later that night he was still scratching. He scratched around his neck and he scratched around his stomach and I told her he must have a bad case of the fleas, but Sarah told me that it couldn't be fleas because she gave him a flea bath when she brought him home earlier. So Mr. King scratched his stomach and he scratched his ears. I told Sarah that maybe we should give him another flea bath and Sarah said okay. I picked up Mr. King and carried him into the bathroom and Sarah started running the bathwater.

The bathwater ran and Mr. King sat on the bathroom floor listening to us. He sat and scratched his ears and I told him it would be okay. Sarah put some flea shampoo in the bath and it got all bubbly and brewing suds. I was getting ready to put King in the bathtub, but then he walked over to the bathroom trash can and lifted his leg and pissed.

"He just pissed on the trashcan," I said.

Sarah turned off the bath and said, "No he didn't."

I said, "Why would I make that up?"

Sarah turned to Mr. King and said, "You're a bad boy, Mr. King. You're a very bad boy." The piss drops rolled down the trash can and onto the floor. I ripped up some toilet paper and wiped the piss off and threw the paper in the toilet. Then Sarah picked him up and put him in the bathtub. I sat and Sarah washed him up and she washed him down. Mr. King opened up his mouth full of his broken off barracuda teeth and breathed deep like he was loving it. He was saying, "Thank you o thank you so much." Then Sarah lathered him up until he became a giant soap ball. She washed his stomach and his legs and his neck and his little pink lipstick popped out again. Sarah repeated, "O gosh Mr. King. You're such a horny boy." I felt jealous the way she was talking to him. Then Sarah rinsed him until the suds slid off and then she put him on the floor. I took a towel and dried him off and Mr. King went crazy. He bashed happy against the sink and then he busted his head against the toilet. "Damn King," I said and finished trying to dry him. Sarah said, "Hopefully that'll help."

But it didn't. The next morning we woke up and King was still scratching. He scratched his neck and he scratched his ear and then he scratched his neck some more. I rubbed my eyes and sat up and then I saw something streaking through his light yellow fur. "What's that?" Sarah said and sat up too. I leaned forward and looked at his neck. It was blood. I said, "Please, Mr. King stop. Please stop scratching buddy. You're hurting yourself." I held his paw down to keep him from scratching but then he started up again. He scratched at his ears and he scratched at his neck and he was whining in this high pitched whine. Sarah got out of bed and started putting on her clothes. She said, "I think I need to take him to the vet." So I sat on the edge of the bed and I felt my legs itching. I scratched around my ankles and Sarah said, "You're not scratching now too are you?" I looked down at my legs and they were covered in bumps. "Fuck," I said. "I have flea bites all over my fucking legs." Then Sarah started scratching around her legs. She looked down and she had red bumps on her skin too and I just shook my head and I told Sarah again we couldn't keep him. This was a disaster.

And this is what I kept saying the next day as I stood outside while Mr. King went pee pee poo poo. Sarah called me from work and I picked up and she told me she had just got a call back from the vet. There was a foot of snow on the ground and King was pissing all over it. Sarah told me that the vet said King didn't have fleas. She told me that he had the mange. And then she told me that we didn't have flea bites either. We needed to take antibiotics though because we had the human form of the mange and it was called scabies. I told her she needed to tell Rebecca that they had to take King back to her dad. I told Sarah we couldn't take care of him, and Sarah finally gave in and said, "I know. I know. I agree."

I told Sarah she had a good heart, but it just wasn't going to work. So I watched King piss in the path I'd shoveled in the snow.

I hung up and when I turned back around I didn't see King anywhere. I walked down the path on the sidewalk that I shoveled and looked for him. Then I walked back to the door and looked that way, but I couldn't find him. Then I walked back down the shoveled sidewalk path and I saw Mr. King down below the house and he was struggling to walk through a snow drift. I walked beside the house where the snow wasn't so deep. I saw him heading towards the hill behind the house and then falling over the hill. He flipped end over end and then rested at the bottom. The snow was blowing and I didn't have gloves on. I shouted, "King. Just stop. I'm coming, King." I stepped into the snow and I felt myself sink down in it and King sat at the foot of the hill in the snow drift and whined for me. "Don't worry King," I said and tried to walk through the snow but it was so deep and drifting that it came up to my waist in places.

I finally found my way to him though. I looked back at where my tracks had left a bunch of leg holes in the snow. I picked him up and told him he was okay now. He was shivering but he still breathed his hot breath and I accidentally swallowed a gulp of it and felt myself gag. He was saying, "Thank you. Thank you for rescuing me." I tried to move forward in the snow but it was so deep and the hill was so steep that I couldn't move. I took a step but I couldn't walk and hold King at the same time. I had to do something.

"Okay, King," I said. "Hold on. I have an idea."

So I pulled him back and tossed him up high into the air in front of me. He landed soft in the snow and then I walked forward and my legs were heavy like tree trunk legs. I picked him up again and threw him a few feet in front of me in the snow drift and he plopped and landed safe in the snow. And so we did this for a half hour until we had made it all the way back up the hill and back to the path I'd shoveled out. I carried him back on the porch and he nuzzled his face against me like he was saying, "Thank you for being kind to me. I'm sorry I'm so blind. I know it's hard for you and I try to be a good boy but it never works out because I live in darkness." I opened the door and put King down on the floor and he shook his fur clean of snow. I kicked off my boots and King looked at me saying, "Please let me stay. Please."

I said, "Why do you want to stay here, Mr. King?"

And Mr. King said, "Because you're kind to the helpless things."

I sat and brushed the snow off of him and I told him he could stay. I called Sarah at work and left a message saying that we needed to keep King and we just couldn't give him back. Then I sat down and I watched him bounce against the walls. I watched him head-butt the couch and I watched him hit his head against the chair. I told Mr. King that he was a metaphor for my life. I told Mr. King he was so helpless and blind and then I told Mr. King that I was a helpless thing too.

We used to do nice things for another though. One night Sarah came home crying because she'd broken an old woman's leg. She told me all you have to do is find a 90 year old woman who weighed 85 pounds and then just move her a little bit. Then you'd see what would happen, you'd see how fragile people are. The next night she came home crying again because a guy had projectile vomited in her mouth and he was HIV positive so she was going to have to take an AIDS test. The night after that she came home and complained about this creepy patient who kept masturbating in front of her. She tried to embarrass him in front of his new girlfriend by asking to change his colostomy bag, but the mad masturbator didn't mind. The new girlfriend didn't either. I told her it would be alright and that everything would be fine and I decided to do something to cheer her up. I looked at the schedule she kept on the side of the fridge and then I counted the number of days she had off this weekend. 1,2,3.

It was getting warmer and winter was almost over. She'd mentioned the beach a few weeks before. So without telling her I got on the computer and I booked a hotel room. I saw the blue water inside my head and I saw Sarah happy. I found restaurants we could eat at and things we could do.

Later that night she went to the bathroom and she shut the door. I thought I heard her crying. I knocked once and then twice.

Sarah whispered, "Scott, I'm in the bathroom." So I went away for a second but then I came back and I slid our hotel reservations beneath the door. I heard Sarah start laughing. "The beach. Thank god. If I had to spend one more day in this shit place, I was going to kill myself."

So we got our shit together for the beach. I imagined the sand and taking pictures of ourselves. I imagined the quiet in the morning and dolphins swimming and the boats on the horizon and then the slow fade until they disappeared.

The night before we were supposed to leave, Sarah called me from work. When she said, "Hello" I could tell something was wrong. She told me that we couldn't go to the beach and then she was quiet. I said it was okay and I asked her why and she told me that we couldn't go to the beach because Becky's father had a heart attack. She told me Becky needed to be with him and that there was no one else to cover Becky's shift. Rhani was out of state and Mindy's daughter was getting married. I told Sarah it was totally okay. I told Sarah that we could do it another time and then I told her we could cancel the hotel reservation and everything would be okay.

But everything wasn't okay. That night Sarah came home and I could tell she was sad. She told me that she had to take a body down to the morgue. It was this little old lady who was so sweet and after she died, Sarah went in and painted the old woman's fingernails because the little old lady always liked it when Sarah painted her fingernails and toenails. But Sarah said she didn't have time to paint the woman's toes. She told this to the funeral home guy who picked her up and he told her it didn't matter because the feet swelled so much after death they usually had to cut off the toes to get them to fit in the shoes for the funeral service. Then the funeral guy laughed and Sarah said she couldn't tell if he was joking or not. She hoped he was joking.

But I told her not worry about it now. I told her everything was okay, but then Sarah said it seemed like no matter what good you tried to do it just turned out wrong in the end. The next morning she woke up feeling so down and went to work like always. I told her we'd go to the beach in the summer and I told her it'd be okay and then I watched her drive away.

After she left that day, I got in my car and I drove to Walmart. It started snowing outside just a little bit and the sun was shining at the same time. But Walmart already had their spring shit out. I took a buggy and wheeled it around and I pushed my cart towards the swimming pool section and then

I shopped. I picked out an inflatable horse to wear around our waists so we wouldn't drown and then I dropped it in the buggy. I picked out an inflatable chicken to wear around our arms and I dropped it in the buggy. I picked out a snorkel and a pair of flip flops and I pulled out a big plastic pool and I balanced it on top of the buggy. I knew I should probably stop but then I drove to Lowes and bought some bags of sand. I felt my arms get heavy from picking them up and putting them in my cart.

I drove home and untied the kiddie pool off the top of the car and I drug it inside and I looked at my watch. I was running out of time before Sarah got home. So I unloaded everything else from the trip and brought it inside. I put the plastic kiddie pool down in the middle of the living room floor and then I popped the bags of sand with my fingertips and poured each plastic bag full of sand into the swimming pool until the sand was ankle deep. I wadded up the empty plastic bags the sand came in and I threw them away. I put on the flip flops I bought and then I blew up the inflatable horse arms like this foooooooo and then I blew up the thingies for my arms like this foooooooooooo. And then I blew up the beach ball I bought. I blew foooo and watched everything grow and then I waited.

That evening Sarah came home from work and I was ready. I put on my sunglasses and then the door opened slow and at first she didn't see me as she unlocked the door, but then she looked up . And this is what she saw: the swimming pool, the sand, the beach ball, the beach.

She saw my swimming trunks and my black socks. And then she started laughing. I told her I hoped she liked the beach and then I took her hand and I said, "Take your shoes off, but be careful because the sand is really hot today." Sarah laughed some more. She kicked off her tennis shoes and then she pulled off both of her socks with her toes. Then she came and stood in the sand and so I took the bucket and we made a sand castle. She kissed me and we looked outside. The snow was spitting a weird spring snow and so I said, "Pretend." And then we saw that the whole world was pretending again.

B ut then a few months later, Sarah came home and she told me the greatest story of all. She told me she was going to have a baby.

I didn't think it could get any worse but it did. I sold my wedding ring one night after Sarah and I signed the papers so my friend Chris and I could go to Lady Godiva's. I went to Cash 4 Gold with my friend Chris and the guy behind the counter looked at my wedding ring and said, "I'll give you 250 dollars for it."

I said, "Sold." I looked at Chris and then I looked at the guy and I asked for 20 dollars in ones. But then Chris decided he didn't want to go. "What do you mean you don't want to go?" I asked.

Chris said, "Well, the last time we went I had a bad time." Of course, the last time we went Chris had just got out of the ER because he'd found out his wife was pregnant with another man's baby and he was threatening to take his own life. We decided to take him to Lady Godiva's and cheer him up, but then one of the dancers had a hemorrhoid and this sent Chris into a suicidal spiral that he never fully recovered from.

I told him it was going to be okay this time and we'd have fun. Then I told him, besides—he should do it for me. I was sick of teaching classes and I was sick of grading papers. I told him about how I saw one of my students on the local news program Crime Stoppers stealing from a Walmart and how some of my students just slept. They were bored with the world and I was bored with them. I was even sick of my ENG 206 classes. I told Chris all the students wanted to do was talk about whether the characters in the stories were good people or bad people or whether the writer was a good person or a bad person. Like this even existed.

Chris pulled up outside the club and the lights glowed from the front of the building and the neon sign. The gravel crackled beneath the track of the tires. There was a sign above the parking lot that said Lady Godiva's. And this was the place. I asked Chris if he had his ID and he said, "Yes."

So we got out of the car and I got my ID out and Chris got out his ID too. We could already hear the boom boom boom coming from inside the building and the walls were vibrating and I felt like we were vibrating too. We walked closer to the door and we tried to recognize the song that was playing on the inside. We wondered what it was and watched a couple of big coal miner looking guys come stumbling out the front door. They looked like they were buzzing and the looks on their faces were like, "Hey if you look at me the wrong way I'll stomp a brand new asshole in the middle of your forehead, boy." I didn't want somebody stomping a brand new asshole in the middle of my forehead so I tried not looking at them and I hoped Chris wasn't looking at them either. We walked up the steps and we opened the front door and entered into a tiny closet sized room with a window and a big door. The hole at the bottom of the window opened up and we couldn't see inside. We heard a muffled voice and we handed over our IDs and then we both waited. The sign next to the window said: NO FIREARMS ALLOWED.

The guy behind the glass slid our IDs back to us like they were puzzle pieces. Then the door buzzed and unlocked and Chris pushed the door open and then the room just popped around us. There was music and there were cigarettes. And there was cigarette smoke. And there were girls with dyed blonde hair in bikinis and heels. And there were dark haired girls and there were big girls and there were stoned girls and everyone was wonderful. And there was a bar and there was a row of people sitting at the bar drinking drinks and drinking beer and there were naked dancers and one was on the stage twirling around and around and upside down and then down on her knees and picking up dollars. There were fat guys at the bar and skinny guys and all kinds of guys. Every type of heart in the world was here and we were all the secret people. We were sons and daughters and mothers and friends and no one could judge us and no one could know us because tonight we were together. Tonight we were alive. There was a dancer in the very back you could only see in the reflection which showed her dancing on a fat dude's lap. And there were dancers standing at the bar and there were dancers sitting at the bar and it was beautiful. Chris and I sat down next to a truck driver looking guy and we ordered two beers and then a dancer walked over and started talking to Chris.

I spun around on the bar stool and looked at the stage. A new girl came on and she spun around and I watched her walk a long walk and fall on all fours like a panther. Then she scissor kicked her legs and pushed her ass towards us. She gave her butt cheek a little smack and the butt cheek bounced and did a tiny ripple shake and then she looked at me and I looked at her.

Then she finished dancing and another girl came out and I felt something drop inside. I recognized her. Or at least I thought I recognized her. She looked like a former student of mine. I spun back around on the bar stool and hoped she didn't recognize me and then I saw her reflection in the mirror above the bar. She had tattoos at the top of her spine and on her shoulder blades were tattoos of cheetah spots or angel wings. So I leaned over and whispered to Chris and I asked if he wanted to leave, but he said we just got here and gave me a look like I was a dumbass. I wondered if I should just go and sit in the car, but I knew Chris would probably be here for a while.

I was just about ready to get up and leave when I heard someone say, "Hey Mr. McClanahan. What are you doing here?" I looked at her and I saw Tiffany. And Tiffany didn't look like she looked at school though. Her hair was all poofed and her eye makeup was put on thick and she sat down next to me and she was holding her cigarettes and a tiny sparkling purse. I took a sip from my beer and she smiled and said, "You should buy me a drink, Mr. McClanahan." And so I did. Then we both laughed and she said, "Well, this is uncomfortable." And then we talked about all of the secret lives we lead and how the true world is hidden from all of us. We both looked at ourselves in the mirror and the dancer spun and twirled on the stage behind us and then I asked her how long she'd been working here and what her stage name was. She looked at me with a fake sexy look and shook her head in a robot shake. Her dark hair tumbled over her shoulders and she whispered, "Misty Lee." Then we both laughed again and she flicked her cigarette and the ashes glowed bright. She told me that she'd worked here for three years and the money really helped to take care of her sick grandmother and her son. She told me how she loved to dance. Then she said, "My Mawmaw is all I've ever had. She's raised me since I was a baby. I'm all she has." Then she smiled and said, "I'm sorry I dropped your class last year. I was having a hard time." I told her it was okay and that she didn't need to worry about it. I was still thinking about leaving.

She said, "I'm sorry to say, but the stuff you gave us to read in class was just so boring." And so I laughed because this was the only criticism I ever understood anyway. This was the only crime: boring people. I told her she was right and then she smiled. She reached out with one hand and touched my leg. I didn't tell her to move it and I didn't talk about the nature of ethical dilemmas. I didn't tell her that my life was falling apart and that I was getting a divorce. I didn't tell her that I was worried Sarah had met someone new and that I'd lost everything in my life. I didn't tell her that I hoped her grandmother would be okay. I just picked at the label on the beer bottle and then she leaned in close to me and said, "So Mr. McClanahan, I have a question for you."

I said, "Yes."

She said, "Do you want to see my pussy tonight?"

Of course, I should have said no. I should have got up and left immediately. But I didn't say no and I didn't get up to leave. I just smiled and nodded my head. And so she grinned and I grinned and she took me by the hand and led me into the back room where the mirrors were. I opened up my legs and she walked around them and between them and over them and stepped like a spider. I thought about the secret world and our secret lives and the lies of our minds. I kept thinking honest thoughts for the first time in a long time. I thought about how I was wearing clothes someone made somewhere in the third world and I didn't care who. I ate fast food and shopped at stores that supported conservative causes and I didn't care. I shopped at stores that were anti-union and I didn't question why the boots I wore only cost 150 dollars instead of 400. I turned on lights and didn't care about where it came from. I paid taxes each year to a country that made bombs to blow people up and I thought horrible thoughts about men and women and children too. I was a horrible person sometimes. Then I smiled and whispered to a world of imaginary people, "And you know what? You are too."

A few weeks after we signed the separation papers, I couldn't sleep. I drank a six pack of beer, but that didn't help either. I flipped and flopped on the cold couch until the couch got hot and then I started to sweat and shake. I tried sleeping on my stomach and then I tried sleeping on my side, but I still couldn't sleep. I tried sleeping on my stomach and then I tried sleeping on my side again and then I tried sleeping on my back, but I started thinking, "You need to go by the house, Scott. You need to go by Sarah's house." So I got up and put on my clothes and tried to find my keys and I found them.

I got in the car and started looking out for cops, but I didn't see any. I drove up the hill to the house where I used to live and I drove down a side street and I parked in the parking lot of the apartment complex that was down from Sarah's. I looked around and stopped across the street and then I went into the woods so I could sneak up behind the street. The moon was out and it was throwing shadows over everything. I kept looking up at the windows of the houses and I was afraid that one of the old women on the street would see me walking through the back yard like a thief and call the cops. I said, "Fucking cops."

I tiptoed up closer to the house and I watched it glow in the darkness. The yellow light was coming from the basement and it was coming from the windows and it was coming from the back of closed doors and glowing in the backyard. I walked closer to the light and that's when I saw it. It was a brownish BMW with a WVU school of medicine license plate parked in the back yard behind our house. On the back of the car was a vanity license plate that said BABYDOC1. It was Dr. Jones' car. I thought about keying his car, but instead I walked closer to the house.

I walked up behind the back door and made sure I stood in the blackness of the night so no one could see me in the light. I looked inside the house. There were two people there. One was Jones and the other was Sarah. They were drinking out of tall glasses and they were talking. They were talking about how strange it is that people meet, how strange it is that we have come together how we have. I was about ready to scream at them that it was all chance, blind chance, and we're only broken mirrors for one another, but then I stopped. I stopped because I noticed something and it was something that I hadn't seen in Sarah's eyes for years or maybe even ever. She looked different now.

She looked happy.

*　　*　　*

But really that night I didn't even think about pulling out my keys and scratching his car. I was drunk and I didn't want there to be a confrontation and I didn't even see Sarah. I ran back to my car after I saw his car and then I drove home. I kept telling myself on the way, "You're almost home. You're almost home." When I got back to my apartment I called Sarah on the phone. It rang and rang and went straight to her voicemail. I hung up and called the house phone. It rang and nobody answered. I hung up and called again. It rang and then finally Sarah picked up. I called her a liar and she called me a selfish dick. I called her a cheater and she called me a cocksucker. I called her a bitch and she told me I was just having my man period like usual. She told me I was horrible and I was. She repeated, "Man period. Man period." I tried to think up something I could say that would make her stop because I couldn't think of any. Finally I thought up something. I said, "I'm going to call your Mom." Then it was quiet and she started laughing. She laughed so much and said, "Scott, can't you come up with anything better than that? I'm 37 years old." I laughed too and then we laughed together, but then I got mad and I told her she was a cheater. She told me we were legally separated now and she knew I'd done worse talking to people online all the time and I was the one who was drunk all of the time and I was the cheater. Then she called me a dick. And I told her she was a whore and she told me I was a piece of shit.

Sarah finally had enough and shouted, "Yes I'm a whore. I have a dick in my hand and a dick in my mouth right now and I have one in my ass and then I'm holding one right now beneath my armpit to keep it warm. I'm sucking a million dicks, Scott. A million. I'm even sucking one right now in the middle of this fight." I told her I hated her and she told me she hated me. Then I hung up on her and I thought about a million dicks. I thought about the million dicks inside my mind.

Right before the divorce date, Sarah and I had to take this child parenting class that was mandated by the state of WV for people who were getting divorced and who had children. The day we showed up, we didn't even talk about our fight from the night before. Sarah just sat in the middle of the child parenting class doing her crossword puzzle and not really caring that it was a waste of time. I didn't have any crossword puzzles though and it was sure as hell bothering me. All I had was this old picture of me sitting on the Easter bunny's lap which I took as a joke for Sarah so long ago. It had just started a fight back then when I left it on her car at work and she thought it was creepy. I said, "Creepy. It's a grown man sitting on the Easter bunny's lap. It's funny. What the fuck you got against the Easter bunny?"

I showed Sarah the picture in the child parenting class now and she just rolled her eyes and said, "Still creepy" and then something about why I'd brought it. Then we both laughed and I put the picture away and I tried not going crazy. "I want to leave," I said. Sarah kept telling me to shut up. We had to be here. It was just a requirement and it would be over soon. So I shut up and listened to the guy who was teaching the class tell his dumb stories and joke his dumb jokes. "Now I know you think your life is over, but I'm here to tell you it's not," he said. "I'm sure you can't even stop thinking about killing your soon to be ex-spouse right now, but that'll change with time." The joke worked and the people in the class laughed. So he kept going. "But there is going to be a time when they'll just become a mild annoyance in your life and you won't even think those thoughts." He paused. "Well you might still think about tripping them and laughing when they fall."

Sarah looked up from her crossword puzzle and laughed at his dumb joke. And then the rest of the class laughed too. I looked around the room and the class looked like the perfect example of why democracy was such a bad idea. "Good god. It's people like these who are the reason I'm pro-choice and pro-epidemic diseases," I said under my breath. I wanted to tell them they were retarded but I knew you couldn't say retarded anymore. Sarah told me to shush and then she grinned.

Then a woman who worked with Sarah at the hospital and who was sitting in front of me raised her hand and asked the man how long it had been since the guy teaching the class had got divorced. The man didn't say anything for a moment and got the video ready. Then he said, "Oh, ma'am. I'm sorry. I've never been divorced. I'm just following the script they gave us." The room stopped laughing and people dropped their heads and then the guy bent down and pushed play on the movie he had to show us and we had to sit through. It was a testimonial movie and full of statistics about what not to do with our children now that we were getting a divorce. The video said that there is a 90 percent failure rate of relationships started before, or during a divorce proceeding. Then there were helpful hints about not letting your baby drink carbonated beverages out of bottles. They called it "Mountain Dew mouth" and it led to tooth decay. They reminded us not to do drugs with our children and then in another testimonial a wife told us about an ex-husband who was giving their baby beer in a bottle and what she did about it.

I whispered to Sarah, "I want to party with a baby."

"Shhh," Sarah said and went back to her crossword puzzle.

I tried to watch the video some more but I was still bored. I decided to try talking Sarah out of the divorce again so we wouldn't have to sit through this class. I told her nobody would ever see her like I did and nobody would love her more than I had. I told her she would probably end up divorcing me three or four times in her life before it was all over. Then the people sitting around us started listening to me and they were all laughing at what I was saying. I noticed that the bailiff over in the corner was watching me. I put my head down and said, "I think the bailiff is looking at me."

Sarah said, "Shh."

When I sat back up, he was still looking at me. It was like he was listening to what we were saying too. But I kept trying to talk Sarah out of the divorce and get her to change her mind. She was still being stubborn though and the bailiff kept watching us.

Then I noticed that the bailiff was standing up. Now he was walking our way. I said, "O shit" and I dropped my head back down like I was hiding my face from him. I could still see the rest of the class watching the TV screen. I looked out of the corner of my eye and I saw Sarah raise her head up and smile. I saw the bailiff's legs walk and then heard his shoes go tap tap across the floor. Then he stopped in front of us and put his hand on his holster. He leaned over and asked Sarah, "Mam, is he bothering you?"

I saw Sarah put her crossword puzzle at her side and she said, "Yes sir, he's been bothering me since I was 24 years old. So you're about 15 years too late in asking."

I sat up in my seat and they both smiled and then he said, "Well, do you want me to move him for you?" Sarah looked at me and then she looked at the officer and then she looked at me and then she looked at the officer and she said, "Why yes. I think I would like that."

The officer motioned for me to stand up, which I did. Then he motioned with his fingers for me to sit on the bench next to the rest of the class and said, "There." I sat where he said and the rest of the class looked at me and they were all whispering to one another. "What's going on? What's happening?" I looked back at Sarah and she was just working on her crossword puzzle and looking like nothing was bothering her. Then she looked at me and stuck her tongue out. And then she smiled. I put my head in my hands and I thought about long ago when we used to make one another laugh. I thought about the children being born. I thought about how I used to sleepwalk and one night wound up in bed with her dad. The next morning she laughed and said she hoped her dad wasn't going to steal her husband away from her. I thought about how we used to laugh and I then I pulled the Easter Bunny picture out of my pocket again and I looked at it. I thought about when Sarah had her gall-bladder removed and when I went to the hospital with her. The admitting nurse was going over her paperwork and said, "And so you're covered by your husband's insurance. Yes?"

I immediately looked at Sarah and said, "Wait! You didn't tell me you were married."

The admitting nurse looked shocked and Sarah looked shocked and I looked shocked, but then Sarah smiled and I smiled and the admitting nurse smiled and everything was fine. I thought about things like this and I kept my head down. Sarah texted me, "I'm sorry he moved you. I thought he could tell I was just joking." I texted her back it was okay and then I watched the rest of the video tell me that we shouldn't fight in front of the children and we shouldn't use the children in our own personal wars. I listened to the video tell me that we were still a family, but we were just a different family now. The video said that we would still love one another, but we would love one another differently. I thought about how I sang lullabies to Iris and Sam and I imagined these lullabies now. I listened to the video and every now and then I picked my head up and looked back at Sarah. It looked like it didn't even bother her really. She was still working on her crossword puzzle.

The video played and the video ended. The guy who taught the class came by with a sign-in sheet. Sarah signed the sheet and then the next person and then the next. He walked over to me and said, "Hey troublemaker." I signed my name and my SS# and my address too. It was the facts of my life, but it didn't tell them anything. I knew that no one wanted to know anything about anything anyway. So I walked to the back of the courtroom and Sarah waited for me. She smiled and said she was sorry again and she didn't think the bailiff was going to move me and I told her it was okay again. And then together we walked.

Sarah asked, "Did you think you'd ever have to sit through a class where someone told you how to raise your children." I smiled and shook my head and then Sarah smiled and shook her head. So we walked down the stairs and out the courthouse doors. I asked her if she remembered my old love letters where I told her she was the dust on butterfly wings. Sarah said, "There's only one thing worse than a love letter with the word butterfly in it and that is a butterfly tattoo. Love letter butterflies and tattooed butterflies should both be avoided at all costs."

I asked her if she remembered the language I created for her in the old love letters that we called the language of Sarah and how my final words one day would come from this language: lipsidipium. Sarah said that no one would know what it means. And I said: "Yes, it'll be just like our time on earth. It'll be just like the Buddhist monk's love letter."

Then we laughed. And nothing seemed to bother her. I asked her if she finished her crossword puzzle and she said, "Getting there." Then we stood on the sidewalk for a second. We gave one another a hug and we said goodbye. She walked to her car and I walked to my car. I repeated again, "It doesn't even bother her."

I got in my car and pulled out. Then I drove down the ramp of the parking garage and on to the street. I circled around the courthouse building and then I circled again. I knew since we filled out the separation papers and completed the child parenting class a divorce date was coming now. And so this was the end. And it didn't bother her.

I listened to the CD player and I rolled down the window. I drove to the red light and then I stopped. I looked out the window at the courthouse and then I looked at the street. Then I looked at the red light. Then I looked at the parking lot and I saw something. I saw Sarah's black Honda CRV. I saw Sarah inside. She had her hands to her face. And she was just sitting in her car and she was weeping. She was wiping away the tears from her face with a wadded up handkerchief and she was trying to stop crying, but still she sobbed. I saw that she wasn't a rock. She was just a person who I had loved and now she was gone. I was gone too.

So I have decided to include a crossword puzzle inside this book because Sarah would have liked that. But this crossword puzzle is different. This is a crossword puzzle that is the hardest crossword puzzle in the world. And you can try to solve it too.

6 across is the name of your first love.

7 down is the name of the one who broke your heart. You belong to them.

2 across is what we have lost.

And then there are other boxes but no answers to go with them. These are the boxes we leave empty.

5 down is what will change for all of us and 1 down is how we will disappear.

S o inside my memory the baby grew inside of her. Then one day Sarah went for a check-up. The baby was almost here. It was just a normal check-up but then she called me crying.

"Scott, they're taking the baby. They're taking her today. I'm on my way to the hospital."

What happened?

The baby wasn't moving and the baby weight was low. Sarah was 35 and a high risk mother. So it would be best to induce her. Now. So we waited all day and then we waited half of the evening. Sarah sent me home at nine that night because they had no idea when the baby would come. I sat and drank in secret and then the phone rang. It was Sarah. She said she needed me after all. She said the baby was coming and she said the doctor said she was fully dilated. I was quiet for a second.

Sarah said, "Scott."

I said, "So a dude had his hand in your vagina?"

I was joking but not really.

Sarah told me this was no time to be jealous and she said she needed me. She needed Bubbies and I was the Bubbies.

I took off and zipped to the hospital and there she was. She was shaking. This wasn't normal shaking. Her hands were shaking and her arms were shaking and her head was shaking and her feet were shaking and her knees were shaking and her legs were shaking and she was shaking. I looked at her again to make sure I was seeing right. Her hands were shaking and her arms were shaking and her head was shaking and her feet were shaking and her knees were shaking and her legs were shaking and she was shaking.

"Are you cold?" I asked.

Sarah smiled and said, "No, Scott. I'm not cold. I'm in pain. I'm in horrible pain."

So Sarah was in pain. Aren't we all? And so I held her hand and sang "No Woman No Cry."

And she smiled. "O god no, Scott. Not fucking reggae."

But it shook me and if I had to tell you about what I know on the nature of birth, it would be this. It would be Sarah McClanahan shaking in the bed and her eyes full of one word. Terror. And then me. Scott McClanahan: The one who was powerless over terror.

The epidural guy came and asked me to leave the room. He explained it was a legal thing, "A liability thing, you know." So

I stood in the hallway and gave Sarah a thumbs up and a silly face.

I looked like this:

But then Sarah smiled. She knew that the only education one needed is this. They should watch someone die and then see someone being born. And then we would know the world. And then the man explained to her she could be paralyzed by the epidural.

Then the epidural guy handed Sarah a pen and she tried to sign. Her hand was so shaky that she had to try three different times.

The document was signed. The epidural was too late. The pain of labor was starting. I thought as I waited, "Fuck you, pain."

And pain said this: Nothing. And rocks said this: Nothing. And rivers said this: Nothing. And the sky said this: Nothing. I said: "I am alive" and then pain said: "This does not create in me a sense of obligation." And even though pain does not have ears to hear I wanted to say it again.

But in my memory Sarah is not in pain. She is sitting up in bed just like she was that afternoon and she is beautiful. She is beautiful because she has two hearts inside her beating, beating.

But then suddenly she is in pain again and her labor has started. Her face is all scrunched up like a poop face or like a fucking face. And I'm there pushing up one knee to her chest and the nurse has the other knee and is pushing it up to Sarah's chest.

So hold her hand.

The doctor and the midwife are down the hallway because there's an emergency. A baby is being born blue and dying with the umbilical cord wrapped around its head. In another room is a premature baby and they're going back and forth, back and forth with "O shit" faces. And here in this room the nurse is looking over at me and I'm looking over at the nurse.

She has a look on her face like, "Are you ready? We're gonna deliver this baby, motherfucker." So my PTSD kicks in and I'm ready for crisis. We're gonna deliver this baby, motherfucker.

The nurse puts the shit bag beneath Sarah and I say "What's that?"

The nurse says, "That's the shit bag." Sarah says all doped up, "That's the shit bag."

Then the nurse whispers, "It's for, ya know? The feces and afterbirth." I'm confused.

The nurse says "Sometimes a woman is pushing so hard that she has put so much pressure on her body that the bowels just give loose. And then of course the afterbirth."

Now I'm thinking, "Sarah. Don't crap in front of these people. We don't know them. It would be rude." And then it's like Sarah is reading my mind because she says, "Don't worry, Bubbies. I gave myself an enema before I came here. That's one good thing about being induced. You can give yourself an enema."

And now Sarah is no longer talking about her enema but she's asking me a question.

"What does it look like?"

I look down at her dilated vagina and a baby head is pushing out.

I answer her like this: "It looks like a wet mole. It looks like you're holding a wet mole between your legs."

The nurse turns her back to us and gloves up.

Then Sarah whispers, "No, how does my pussy look?"

At first I'm thinking, "What a weird question," but then I get what she's saying. I look back between her legs again and I say.

It looks sort of angry.

"No tearing?" she asks.

Tearing?

I didn't even know they could tear, but they can. They can tear into one giant tear.

I said, "No, I don't think."

"What about my wax?"

What?

"I waxed myself a few days ago knowing I was going to be showing off my stuff. I know how nurses are. Didn't want anybody talking about my stuff and how it looked like a mop."

Then she was quiet.

Then Sarah said, "So my pussy looks angry?"

I said, "Yeah, your pussy looks angry."

But enough about suffering. Back to birth. So Sarah is pushing. Pushing. Pushing. Pushing. And then she breathes. Then she is pushing pushing pushing pushing pushing pushing pushing. And then she rests. And then she is pushing. Pushing. Pushing. Pushing and then there is screaming. A baby is pushing her arm out of the vagina and looking at us with a fucked up baby looking face. She has a look like I'm pushing my way out of a vagina, buddy. What are you looking at? The baby groans eeeeee, and then this happens. There's a lightning storm outside. It's smashing and crashing around us and cutting through the dark and the baby girl is pulled from the womb and given to her mother and then there is one more lightning bolt that goes Boom.

We see the baby glowing and flashing and on fire, sparkling like flashers beside a fatal accident. The lights go out and then they come back on, and when they do the little girl has a lightning bolt on her nose. She is crying. Her name is Iris.

We are alive.

That night I sat and watched the History channel documentaries about long ago. Sarah rested in the hospital with the baby and I watched the stories of the Macedonian phalanx and the rolling rumble of death. I watched how Alexander cried when he was a boy because his father was victorious and would leave him nothing to conquer. I watched the story of the Battle of Cannae and how 50,000 men were killed in a single afternoon. 100 each minute. I watched the soldiers of Napoleon rage their way across Europe. I watched the stories of how soldiers were trapped in the rocks of Gettysburg and their eardrums exploded from the sheer noise. I watched how 100,000 and then 200,000 and then 300,000 and then 400,000 and then 500,000 and then 600,000 died on this ground beneath us. I watched the stories of the World Wars and how more people were killed in the 20th century than all of the other centuries combined. I watched documentaries on Mao and Hitler and Stalin and the Gulag. I watched the story of the battle of Stalingrad and a million more dead. I watched the story of the dropping of bombs and mushroom clouds and 90,000 dead in a single afternoon and how many of their shadows were left on sidewalks after they were vaporized. I watched the same death pour through it all and the skeletons and the bodies of zombies rose like mountains. And they were all in love with something. And I wondered if these wars were love letters of some sort. Love letters that said nothing.

PART III

We started calling the place we lived the apartment of death. My friend Chris moved in with me because he was going through a divorce too. So it was a real cheerful place to live. One night we were sitting around and Chris was going on about how our wives were probably on drugs and this is why they were divorcing us. "Like seriously on drugs. Seriously. Either that or fucking nervous breakdowns." I laughed and said, "Yeah it has nothing to do with us." I was drinking and watching YouTube clips over and over again. My record was watching the Guns N Roses "November Rain" video fourteen times in a row before Chris begged me to stop.

And nothing lasts forever even cold November rain.
And nothing lasts forever even cold November rain.
And nothing lasts forever even cold November rain.
And nothing lasts forever even cold November rain.

But then we heard something out behind the apartment and it sounded like bottles breaking or somebody shuffling something around next to the dumpsters.

I went and looked out the window at the dumpster behind the apartment. It was dark and snowing and the snow glowed golden beneath the street light. I didn't see anything so I walked back into the living room and Chris started doing this character he always did called the dumb racist. It was this guy who always watched TV and made racist comments but he was so dumb he always got his stereotypes mixed up. The dumb racist was not to be confused with another character Chris did called the racist spider who was a spider but was also a racist.

I sat back down at my seat and the dumb racist said, "Those fucking Irish micks with their big dicks." And then. "Yeah whatever. Those Native Americans sure can do some fucking math."

I laughed a little but then I heard the clinking outside in the trash again.

I went over to the window and looked out once more. Snow was covering everything but then I saw something moving in the snow at the bottom of the green dumpster. I saw 1,2,3,4,5 kittens just like that.

"What is it?" Chris said.

I said, "Kittens. It's a bunch of kittens and they're hungry." So I went to the fridge but all I could find was a bottle of ketchup and some beer. We had hot dogs in the bottom of the fridge from when I first moved in and they looked disgusting but I thought it would be okay. So I went outside in the snow and all of the kittens took off running. The snow was falling down from the streetlight and I took the wieners and I broke them up into chunks and then I threw them on the ground. They disappeared into the snow. "Where's the mother?" Chris asked. I told him I didn't know and then we went back inside and turned the lights off. We waited and watched the kittens come back and I said, "Maybe they don't have a mommy. Maybe they are orphans like us." I pointed out how the kittens were all solid black except one. The one who wasn't black had a white neck and face.

The next morning I put the hot dogs out for the kittens and walked away. And again the kittens came scrambling to eat the hot dog chunks out of the snow. I had an idea. We went out that evening to buy the kittens the best food I could afford, but instead I decided to pretend I was a bunny first and buy some beer. "What do you mean?" Chris said. I told him he was going to tape me with his phone and I was going to pretend being a bunny. So Chris laughed and I laughed and he got out his phone and hit record. I stood outside the gas station and he pointed his phone at me.

I put my hands up in a bunny pose and I said in a child's voice. "I'm a bunny. I'm a bunny."

Then I started hopping.

I hopped inside the store and I hopped by the customers getting coffee and I hopped past the candy and potato chips and then I hopped into the beer cooler. I said, "I'm a bunny." And then I took the beer with my little bunny arms and hopped over to the counter and bought the beer. The girl behind the counter said, "What are you?" I told her, "I'm a bunny." Then she looked at me like she was scared, but I thought that was silly because bunnies don't rob gas stations and kill people.

We put the beer in the car and then I walked over to Kroger. I stopped pretending to be a bunny and Chris stopped filming me as I pretended to be a bunny because we had kitty supplies to buy. So we went and found the meat section and I looked out at the whole aisle of meat. There were sirloin steaks and there were ribeye steaks and pork loin and rump roasts of beef. Eenie meenie minie moe. I finally picked up two thick Black Angus steaks and Chris just shook his head. I asked him if the steaks didn't look good or something and Chris just shook his head and told me we couldn't buy steaks for kittens. Kittens couldn't eat steak. I said, "Oh yeah" and then I put them back. He told me we should look for hamburger then. We looked through the stacks of hamburger until we found a pack of expensive, organic hamburger patties that cost 12 bucks together. I told Chris that this was perfect and then we started for the front of the store. But then my phone rang.

It was my father. I picked it up and my father asked me what I was doing. I told him that Chris and I had found some orphaned kittens and I was going to buy some nice hamburger for them. My dad said, "I don't think a guy with money problems should be buying expensive hamburger for kittens. Do you?" I'd had about enough of his shit so I got mad and said, "Daddy, I only buy the best for my kittens." Then I hung up.

Chris didn't know what to say. I paid for the hamburger like I always did with everything. I paid with a credit card and I told Chris that I liked paying for things with a credit card because it felt like life. Credit cards were like hearts. One day someone would come collect on our debt of life and the ones with the largest debts had lived the deepest lives. I was down 44,000 dollars by this point and I was getting cut off now.

We went home and Chris cooked the hamburger for me. We mushed it up with a fork and then we put it on a small plate and we took it outside and set it down next to the dumpster and then we went inside. We waited and watched out the window and we didn't see anything. But then Chris said, "Look." Slowly the little kittens started to appear. They moved like dots against the snow and started to eat. We watched them and we grinned like children. The snow was falling again and we didn't talk about what had been going on. We didn't talk about how Chris' wife was pregnant with another man's baby. We didn't talk about the night he got sent to the hospital because he was suicidal. We didn't talk about how a few weeks after he moved in I was passed out upstairs and I didn't hear him knocking on the door outside the apartment because I'd locked him out.

An hour or two later when he came back, I started crying. I begged him not to die. Then we went to see a movie and I cried through the whole thing. We joked about it a few weeks later as our night of apocalypse, but we didn't think about this night of apocalypse. We just watched the kittens eat and then the next day we fed them the same and the day after that. I talked about it with friends so they would think I was a good person. This is what people do.

The next day I woke up and I was late. I didn't have time to put the hamburger out for the kittens. I put my clothes on and got out to my car. I looked over at the plate in front of the dumpster and it was empty. I started up my car to let it warm up and then I pulled out the scraper to scrape off all of the ice. I went scrape scrape scrape on the front window and then I moved to the side and went scrape scrape scrape. I put my hands up to my mouth and I tried to blow them warm, but my breath blew out like a ghost. Then I got in the car and threw the scraper in the back. I started to back up towards the dumpster and then I saw a streak of black pass by. I felt a tiny bump, bump. I stopped the car and got out and I walked over to the dumpster.

I stood over the dead kitten. It's hind legs were shaking shake, shake. It shook some more like it was doing some strange death dance. And then it stopped. It was the kitten with the white face. I named it Blackie. So I was going to bury it but then I realized I was going to be late for work. I couldn't be late for work because I'd been late for work a lot recently. So I got back in my car and told myself I'd come back and bury it later. But when I came back that evening it'd already been run over again. The garbage truck had picked up the dumpster and now the kitten was crushed flat. I didn't do anything. This is how nothing takes care of nothing.

I made it a new monument that evening. A true one. When I came home again the next evening I whipped the wheel wide and I ran over the kitten lump. The next morning I backed up and watched the dumpster grow larger. I ran over this death. The morning after that I came back home and ran over it again. Then the next day I ran over it once more and I knew if I ran over it enough then maybe one day it would all be gone.

I thought we were going to get robbed. Chris and I had been living in the apartment behind the mosque for a month now and people were getting robbed all the time. One night we were coming back from eating chicken wings when we saw this guy hanging out in the mosque parking lot. "Fucking meth heads," I said as we pulled into our parking spot in front of the apartment building. I had just been telling Chris about how I caught this woman going through our mailbox that day and stealing our Captain D's coupons. "Fucking coupons," I said. "You don't mess with a man's coupons."

Chris put the car into park and looked back at the weird guy in the parking lot. He was just standing back there watching us. "See, he's probably just waiting for us to get out of the car or he's already stolen a bunch of our shit." Chris laughed and asked me what we even had in our apartment that they could steal. I told him I had all of my books packed up in boxes. 5,000 volumes. The greatest small volume library in the state. Chris looked at me and said, "Yeah I hear people are trading stolen copies of St. Augustine's *Confessions* for pills all the time now." I didn't pay any attention to him and told him that they better not steal my Sid the Science Kid DVDs. "I need those DVDs when the kids come over." Then I sang the song, "I got a lot of questions and big ideas, I'm Sid the Science Kid."

But Chris didn't laugh. He turned the engine off and the headlights disappeared and the front of the building became black. Chris was just about ready to get out of the car when I stopped him. "No. Just wait. That guy is still back there." Then I watched the guy standing in the parking lot and watching us still. The guy looked nervous too and kept looking around. "I don't know," I said, but then Chris got out of the car.

"No. No. No. Don't," I said but Chris was already out of the car. So I got out of the car too even though I didn't want to. I picked up my plastic bag with the six pack inside and shut the door behind me. I looked up at the apartment window where Diablo Jr. lived. I thought if we had problems I could shout for him to help us. Diablo Jr. was a local professional wrestler who was always fucking this fat woman who lived next door.

Chris shut his door and walked around to the car and watched the guy. Chris hit the lock button on his keychain and the lock locked and the lights on the car flashed and locked again. The horn honked honk. Then I walked to the back of the car and watched the guy. He still kept looking around, but then I remembered I'd forgotten my chicken wings. I had Chris unlock the door again. I reached in and picked the box of chicken wings out. "You've even made me paranoid," Chris said, looking around. And then I said, "You know what happens if you look up the word paranoid in the dictionary? It's the same as cynicism: A deep and profound understanding of human nature." So Chris and I started to walk. We only had a key to the back door so we had to walk around to the back of the apartment building. That's when we saw the guy following us.

"Fuck. He's following us," I told Chris and we started walking faster. Chris walked even faster and passed me and then I tried to walk faster too and catch up with him. I heard footsteps stomping fast behind us. The guy was walking faster too. "Fuck," I said. Chris looked back and then I looked back too. Chris took his keys out of his pockets to have them ready to unlock the door. But the footsteps kept following us and so Chris walked faster and then I walked faster too like I needed to go to the bathroom really bad. But I couldn't keep up with Chris and felt jealous because Chris was a faster walker than I was. The guy was still following us.

I saw inside my head the TV headline and news story: *Two divorced dads were robbed at gunpoint last night. The loneliness and desperation of their lives were made small compared to the desperation and loneliness of another. Authorities say the only thing missing from their pathetic apartment of death was a copy of St. Augustine's Confessions and a number of children's TV show DVDs.*

I looked back and the guy was still following us except he was shouting something.

"You have the key?" I asked.

Chris said, "Yes, yes" and the keys kept jangling from his hand and pointed out like a knife. Then we were at our porch and then we were up the steps and at the door, but it was too late. The robber was standing next to us. It was so dark I couldn't see his face. The robber said something but I couldn't hear what he said. I watched his hands to see if he had a knife or a gun, but I didn't see any.

I shouted scared, "What do you want?"

The guy said, "Asalamalakim."

Then Chris and I looked at each other and we laughed at how stupid and scared we were. He wasn't here to rob us. He was just one of those strange things you call friendly and he was wishing us welcome and peace.

He said, "I'm sorry to bother you and I hope I didn't scare you, but do you have the keys to the mosque?" He continued, "Someone was supposed to meet me here tonight and unlock the mosque for me. The Imam said the person with the key lived in the apartments behind the mosque."

I shook my head no and told him it wasn't us.

Chris kept chuckling at how stupid we were and then the guy said, "Well since I have you gentlemen here. I would like to invite you to stop by the mosque this Friday afternoon for our first community welcome event."

He told us there would be food and fellowship and we were both invited. Then he asked if I was a father.

I said, "Sort of" and he told me to bring my children. He told us they would have what they call a "jump house" for the children. He thanked us and we thanked him and we parted.

Chris and I went inside the apartment and we both laughed our asses off at how we thought we were getting robbed. Chris told me that I was like an old woman I was so paranoid. I laughed and told Chris maybe we should go. There were other things we should do too like actually getting a garbage can instead of just having a trash bag hanging off the door of the closet. Maybe I should finally organize all of my boxes of books or at least move them out of the closet and into a storage space. Maybe I should go back to the psychiatrist and change my medicine or actually get something to help me sleep. I thought, "Sleep. O if I could only sleep." Then maybe we should tear down our Ike Turner shrine. Our friend Kendra was coming to visit us soon and we knew she wouldn't put up with an Ike Turner shrine. But perhaps tonight. For tonight maybe someone was trying to tell me something.

The man had come into our minds like a thief in the night and asked questions I'd never asked before. Do you have the keys to the mosque? I laughed and told Chris that someone was trying to tell me something. Chris said, "Who?" I said, "God. The one of many names." I imagined a pilgrimage I would be taking soon. So Chris and I said goodnight like we did every night. We said goodnight like we were both going to bed when in reality we would simply sit on our beds behind closed doors and pretend we weren't alone. But being alone was what we were good at now. That and self-pity. Chris shut his door and I shut my door too and then I turned on my computer. Chris sent me a few texts about the name of someone he was trying to think of when we were eating chicken wings.

I went to the DVD player and put on my Sid the Science Kid DVD and turned off the lights. I sang the Sid the Science Kid theme song, "I got a lot of questions and big ideas. I'm Sid the Science Kid." I took my medicine and sat on my bed and bundled all of the pillows beside me and pretended they were little kids. My kids. I did this sometimes when I was lonely and missing them. I watched Sid the Science Kid and pretended they were here. Sometimes I'd say, "Only three days until I see them" or, "Only two days until I see them." Or, "Only one day, Tomorrow." That one day would be tomorrow soon. I sang along with Sid the Science Kid and I started to ask him questions and Sid the Science kid said things back to me.

I said, "Sid, why do you continue on your Faustian search for knowledge?"

Sid laughed and said, "For wisdom and empirical evidence that even children can understand."

I said, "And what have you discovered in this search?"

Sid said, "Only one thing. We're orphans." Then I wasn't talking to Sid the Science Kid anymore.

I was googling the word "mosque." The website said the word "mosque" came from an original Arabic word which meant: place of worship. I thought about how my only tender mercy now was watching the families arrive at the mosque. So I stayed up all night trying to sleep but not sleeping until I awoke the next afternoon just an hour before my kids were supposed to be here. I rushed around trying to clean up the place and wait for their arrival. It was then that I heard children playing and cars pulling up in the parking lot outside. I looked in between the blinds and I saw a parking lot full of Mercedes and nice cars and then I saw a few children playing in the jump house outside the mosque. There were fathers and there were mothers and there were teenagers. There were a couple of tables too, full of food. The people were sitting around the table and eating and fellowshipping with one another. I saw the wrestler Diablo Jr. He was shaking hands and smiling and showing the kids some wrestling moves. There was the meth looking lady I caught stealing our coupons from the mailbox. She was eating and smiling and I wasn't mad at her anymore. The families were all laughing and the children were running around jumping in and out of the jump house. They all had something I didn't have in my life. They had love and happiness. They could say, "Asalamalakim" and mean it, but I only wanted one thing from them now. I wanted to rob them.

A few weeks later, I spit on Big Ugly's BMW. I always called Sarah's boyfriend Big Ugly now. For weeks now whenever I saw Sarah's boyfriend's car I blew him a kiss. I saw him driving towards the hospital one morning and blew him a kiss. I got behind his car on my way to work one morning and I blew him a kiss. "Would you please stop blowing kisses at Dr. Jones when you're in public?" Sarah asked me on the phone one day. I told Sarah I didn't know what she was talking about. I told her I was a man of peace and blowing kisses was my thing.

Then I said Big Ugly this and I said Big Ugly that. Sarah asked me to quit calling him Big Ugly and wondered why I kept doing it. I told her, "Well he's big and he's also ugly." Then one night I was dropping the kids off at the house and I saw the BMW. I recognized it by the vanity license plate. BABYDOC1. "What a dumb fucking vanity license plate," I said. "You can't trust people with vanity license plates." The car was parked in front of the house and for some reason I just lost it. The snow was falling in big hunks and chunks. I stopped the car and just sat there. The kids were inside my car in the backseat and Sam was about halfway asleep and Iris was kicking her feet against the back of my seat. I looked over at the BMW and then I said, "I'm gonna spit on that car." I opened the back door of my car and got Sam out of the car carrier. I held the handle of his baby carrier seat and walked over to the BMW and just stood there. The snow was falling on Sam's forehead and melting on his skin. I saw Sarah come to the door and stand in the glow of the light. Then I leaned back and hawked a big ass loogie. I felt it fill my mouth full of warmth. Then I let the loogie sit there on my tongue before I launched it high in the air like a rocket ship. It shot off my tongue tip and lips and sailed high in the air, sailing up high into the air and shooting past the snowflakes until it shined silver in the light from the street lamps and glowed. Then it fell down, down, down until it plopped back into the snow pile on the hood of the BMW. "Fucking Nazi car," I said. Then I walked down the front yard and left a path of little angel footprints behind me.

I walked onto the porch and kicked my boots free of snow. Then I opened the door and put Sam inside. "I just spit on your boyfriend's car," I said to Sarah and then walked away to get Iris and bring her inside too.

"Huh," Sarah said. "What did you say?"

Then she asked me again as I walked out. "I said I just spit on your boyfriend's car." Then I walked and followed my footprints in the front yard to the car. I left another set of footprints in the snow beside them until it looked like two different people had been walking there. I opened the door and tried to get Iris out of the backseat. I pushed down the button on the car seat and then I pulled at it but the buckle wouldn't come loose. I pushed down on the button on the car seat again and then I pulled. "Shit," I said "shit." I finally got Iris out of the car seat and then I carried her through the snow and down to the house. She said, "My pack back."

"O shit," I said. "I forgot about the kids' backpack." So I went back to the car and got the backpack.

Then I walked back through the snow.

I sat it down inside the front door and Sarah said, "That's really shitty of you spitting on somebody's car. I don't care who it is."

I told Sarah she used the word "shit" in front of the children and she was a bad person. But then I thought of something else to say. I told her, "Well it's real shitty dating a guy who drives a BMW. Doesn't he know that's a Nazi car?" She told me she didn't care and I wouldn't even know that if I didn't see it on television.

I told her, "What? You don't care about history." I told her that was the problem with people in this day and age. They didn't care about history. Sarah looked confused and then she said, "For fuck's sake, Scott. What the hell does this have to do with history?" I looked at her and I knew she'd divorce me soon.

I didn't say anything for a couple of minutes but then I had an idea. I walked back to the door and Sarah said, "What are you doing?"

I told her, "I'm going to go spit on your boyfriend's car again." So I shut the door behind me and Sarah followed me.

I saw Iris behind the glass mouthing, "What?" Then I realized I left the kid's back pack on the porch when I put Iris inside. So I grabbed it and opened back up the door. Iris started running towards me like I was coming back inside. She put her arms up like she always did because she wanted me to pick her up. But instead of picking her up, I just put the backpack down and then I reached out with my hand to stop her. She was running straight at me and toddler fast. Then my fingertips popped against her chest bone and she stopped. It looked like I'd punched her almost. And Iris' face looked like this.

I'm alone.

So Iris looked confused and Sarah looked confused. I shut the door and walked back up to the BMW at the top of the yard. I traced my tracks on my way up there and I looked back down at the house and I saw Sarah standing in the doorway. She was standing with a baby on her hip and a toddler at her knee. Then I looked down at the vanity license plate. BABYDOC1. I hawked up some phlegm and then I threw back my head and I spit. The spit shot forward and disappeared in the snow in the car. Then I raised my hands high in victory and looked towards Sarah. She had a look on her face like she couldn't believe it. She was shaking her head like, "What's wrong with you?"

I couldn't say.

I went home and I told Chris I spit on a BMW and I did it for us and I did it for the lonely people. Chris didn't know what I was talking about. I told him I was a junkyard dog. I was the junkyard dog of the world and free, but nothing is free.

The next morning I decided to do better. I decided not to blow kisses at Big Ugly and I decided not to comment on how vanity plates were tacky or how it was even worse when the vanity license plate said BABYDOC1: the nickname of the worst dictator in Haitian history. I laughed to myself thinking what I would tell Sarah about other possible vanity plates her boyfriend could get such as Idiamindada1 or better yet go4pol-pot1. I imagined Baby Doc with a giant machete cutting off the hands of the children of Haiti and then high fiving the cut off hands of the children together. I imagined the Haitian people starving.

So I got mad and that afternoon I got drunk. It was snowing outside and there was ice and sleet all over. I started swaying back and forth. The hospital where Sarah worked was just across the road from my apartment. I wandered outside and started walking through the slush of the parking lot of my apartment and then to the road. I watched the cars and trucks and cars coming in front of me. I looked left and I looked right. Left, right, left, right. I was a little kid. Then I took off running across the street and hopped the ditch. Yee haw. I started searching for Big Ugly's car and mumbling. "Where's that shit ass BMW?" I walked down the road and passed Chryslers and Toyotas and Mercedes and pickup trucks and mini vans, but not a BMW. Then I walked around behind the hospital and looked for the car. Most of the cars there were covered in snow now and so it was hard to find. There was a nurse or someone who worked at the hospital smoking a cigarette in her car.

She was watching me. I thought, "Where in the fuck is it?" The snow kept coming down, but then I saw it. The BMW. I walked towards the car and thought about whether I should key it or spit on it or just throw a rock through the window. But I didn't do any of these things. I just stood beside his car and then I walked forward. I swept the snow away from the window and I looked inside. In the front seat was a picture, but I couldn't quite tell what it was. I looked closer and I saw that it was Jones and his son. His son was wearing a Boy Scout uniform and Dr. Jones was wearing a Boy Scout uniform too and they both looked silly. They were both smiling. The son looked like he was about ten years old and he looked like he loved his father more than anything. He looked like he was happy to have his father there. The little boy was holding a trophy and his dad had his arm around him. His dad was a good dad and the son was a good son. But there was a look of sadness in the little boy face as well. It was a look like he knew his daddy would have to leave soon and go away.

And Dr. Jones looked different too. He was smiling but his eyes were sad. He looked like he knew that we only exist in the stories of others and we are all the breaker of horses. And perhaps something else too. Perhaps that an enemy is never an enemy for long, but also a secret friend. He looked like he was dying because he lived far away from his child and only visited every other weekend. He was far away from his child and if there was someone who knew the pain inside of my secret heart it was probably him. He looked like he loved the children and the children looked like they loved him and he was there and he was with them. But inside of this photograph he looked like he was hiding all of his pain. And so I saw the face in the photograph wasn't his face anymore. But it had been replaced by another face and he looked different somehow. He looked like someone who I loved from long ago and he looked like someone I knew once, but who I hadn't seen in years.

That night I sat and watched a movie and tried not to think about what had happened. I watched a movie about an old couple who travelled to Tokyo to see their children. But when they got there, their children were too busy to hang out with them. So on the way back, the mother got sick and the children had to make a journey of their own to sit by the deathbed of their mother and watch her die. The mother died and at the end of the film a neighbor walked by and asked the father how he was doing. The father was alone now and he just sat and looked out at the sea and he said if he knew things would have turned out this way he would have been different.

And now years later I can only think the same thing myself. If I knew things would have turned out like this I would have been different. If I knew things would have turned out like this, I would have been nicer.

After a while Sarah's job started getting to her. We still did nice things for one another though. It was Christmas two years before the divorce and she had to work a 12 hour shift Christmas day and so we decided to open up our presents on Christmas Eve. We sat under the Christmas tree with all the lights off except for the Christmas tree lights and we made a little pile of our presents in front of us. We talked about how opening presents on Christmas Eve always sucked. Sarah seemed sad. Her grandfather had just died a few months before and there was a teenage girl at the hospital who tried to commit suicide by setting herself on fire. Sarah had to listen to her groan all night until she finally died. And her favorite patient, the little old man she called the pirate, wasn't doing too well either. Sarah watched him rip out a catheter two times in a row until his penis became a frayed rope and bled like a hose. That night I sat and listened to Sarah tell me about how her grandfather used to dress up like Santa Claus when she was a little girl. She told me how she used to visit him in the summer at the lake in Michigan and she told me about her memories when she was a little girl.

Then Sarah started opening up her presents. She opened up the purse she already knew about and then she opened up the straightening iron she already knew about. She said, "Hell yeah. It's a straightening iron." She said this like she had no idea what the present was before she started opening it and then she opened up another and said, "O it's a new purse. Yaaay. How did I know?" Then she smiled a smile like she wasn't the one who picked the purse out.

I opened up a couple of CDs and then I opened up a new watch she bought me. I said, "O CDs" and, "O it's a new watch." Sarah told me she was going to get me concert tickets for a singer I liked, but after a couple of weeks she realized why she couldn't find any concert dates. The singer had been dead for years. We laughed together and Sarah's eyes shined, but then she looked sad again. She looked above the fireplace where an urn sat on the mantelpiece. It was an urn containing the ashes of a patient who had died at work. The patient was a seventy year old mentally retarded man who didn't have any family left to claim his remains. So Sarah brought them home one night so that they wouldn't just be disposed of by the state. "People are so alone," she said and then her eyes filled full of tears. We fought when Sarah had brought the ashes home a few weeks before. I told her it was weird as hell and I didn't want some weird dead dude's ashes in the house. "Selfish ass dead people," I said, but Sarah brought them home anyway.

I patted Sarah's leg and told her that I was glad she brought the ashes home. Then I asked her what she was thinking. She told me that she kept thinking about how her grandfather dressed up like Santa Claus when she was a little girl and how no one was going to know it or even think about it except for her. It was her memory and it belonged only to her and then she cried a little bit and she told me that she thought it was cruel how everything changes. She told me how cruel memories and stories and people are. She told me the week before a patient had called Dr. Jones the 'N' word right to his face. I asked her how he dealt with it and she told me he was professional. He did his job. I told her I was sorry and then she apologized for getting sad but she said that she guessed that's what holidays were for. She laughed and asked what it all meant and she said it didn't make any sense and then she asked me what it meant again and why we were cruel.

I told her I didn't know.

That night we fell asleep on the couch and then we woke up a few hours later to the sound of Sarah's alarm on her phone. She put on her scrubs in silence and she put on her makeup in silence. She put on her sweatshirt and then she whispered for me to go back to sleep.

She whispered: "It's Christmas morning, Scott."

But when I woke back up a few hours later I felt nervous. I was all alone and the house was cold. I kept thinking of old men dressed up like Santa Claus. I kept thinking of Sarah when she got the telephone call that her grandfather had died and I thought about Sarah walking around in the front yard and the way she put her hand up to her face and then the way her face scrunched and how there were teardrops hanging on her chin like a little chin beard of tears. I thought about how I had tried to comfort her and I thought about Sarah's face in the Christmas lights and how I wanted to cheer her up when she got home from work. I wanted to surprise her.

I gathered up this stuffed animal that her grandfather gave her long ago. Then I picked a picture of her grandmother that always sat on the desk. She died when Sarah's father was young and so Sarah never knew her except in pictures and stories. I found a photograph of her cousin Ashley who died in a car accident when Sarah was a teenager. I found a photograph of Sarah with her pirate patient right after he'd lost his leg. I took everything I found and I went downstairs where Sarah kept her craft table and all of her wrapping paper. I put them in the Christmas boxes and I wrapped them up new again. I wrapped them up like they'd never been given before.

Then I wrote little notes on each of them.

I wrote notes like this: From Grandpa. To Sarah:

I just wanted to let you know that I'll always love you. And there's still a part of me with you. If you look in the mirror—then I am there. Merry Christmas.

Then I wrote a note from the pirate.

Thank you for being a nurse. It's always good when your job is taking care of people and we need more people who take care of people. Thank you for taking care of me.

Then I wrote one from her grandmother that said, *I know you never met me because I passed away before you were born, but I've always loved you.*

I put the gifts from the past beneath the Christmas tree and waited for Sarah to come home. Sarah called like she always did before she left work and she asked if I wanted anything from Wendy's. I told her no. That evening she was in a shitty mood when she got home. I shouted, "Merry Christmas" and asked her how her day was. I jumped up and down. Up and down. She said, "It was quiet. But I think I was just so tired from staying up last night." I told her not to think about it and I led her over to the Christmas tree and I showed her the wrapped up presents. She told me that she thought we opened up presents the night before, but then I told her that these were the presents from long ago. These were her surprises for the day. I told her that these were the presents from the people of the past who wanted to wish her Merry Christmas again.

Sarah opened one from the pirate who told her "Merry Christmas," and thanks for being a good nurse and that he missed her. Then she opened one from her grandmother who told her that she knew she never met Sarah but she wanted her to know that she always loved her. *Perhaps we love what we never know most of all.* Then grandmother's note: *I hear that you're thinking about having a baby one day and if it's a girl baby—you're thinking of naming her Iris after my own little baby girl who died when she was just an infant. I hope you know that would make me proud.*

And then the note finished like this:

I want you to know that there IS another world. You are right. Scott is wrong. It's a world that surrounds us and we're all together just like right now. All the living and the dead. Sarah smiled and then I gave her a present from her grandfather. It was a stuffed animal he gave her long ago when she was a little girl. Sarah opened up the present and read what it said and then she cried and cried some more. Snot was coming out of her nose. I told her it was okay and that her grandfather loved her and it was okay to miss people.

Sarah stopped crying and told me to shut up and I didn't understand. I didn't understand what she meant. She told me that my Christmas was creepy and that she didn't really know her grandfather that well. She told me that she had bad memories of him and he used to call her brother Jack fat and make comments about her own weight and the way she talked. He didn't want her to get a West Virginia accent. Sarah told me that when he re-married he put a few phrases in the pre-nup where he wanted his second wife to fix him omelets and mimosas three times a week and serve it to him in bed. I just shook my head and told her it must have been a joke and he must have been joking. Sarah said it wasn't a joke. Then she told me that his second wife told her one day that a woman should always marry three times. The first marriage should be for money. The second marriage should be for good looks to pass on to your offspring. The last marriage should be for love. Love should come last. The woman told Sarah that you could tell a lot about a person by whether or not they followed these rules. Then Sarah told me that she found out the patient she called the pirate was a convicted pedophile and that's why his family never visited him and that's why he was alone. She told me Rhani showed her his picture on the West Virginia sex offender computer data base.

Sarah wiped the snot from her nose and walked away. She wanted to go to bed. She was tired.

I'd ruined Christmas.

Then I saw that there are other presents. And they are full of nothing.

They have notes attached that say: *There is not another world. There is only this one. Your memories are just the dumb voices inside your head. Love is just biology and the urges of animals to pass on their genes like rats.* There are others from grandmothers who say: *We just wind up ashes in a stranger's home. Unwanted and unknown.* Others from mothers who say: *You were always annoying.* There is another from your father who writes: *Thank god, I'm dead. We were never close. And we never knew one another. Never.*

And these are the true presents.

This is the real past.

In the days that followed, Sarah watched the things she loved grow older and die. Miss K. was this 80 year old woman who Sarah asked one day what the key to a successful marriage was. Miss K. thought for a moment and then she said, "Two things. The first thing. Keep your damn mouth shut."

"And what's the second thing, Miss K?"

Miss K. said, "Fucking, fucking and more fucking." Sarah blushed hearing these words come out of an 80 year old woman. Miss K. said, "If you can fit together when you fuck, then you'll have a lifetime of happiness."

That weekend Sarah told me about how she decided to check on Miss K. again and see if she needed her hair done, but she had a visitor. It was a man in his 60s with gray hair. Sarah went to check on her after that and there was another man there now. He already had her sitting up on the potty chair and he already had her hair fixed. Later that evening Sarah noticed a different man and he was filing Miss K's fingernails. Sarah noticed yet another man on the final visiting hour and he was reading to her a book of love poems.

"You sure do have a lot of visitors," Sarah said to Miss K. who had been a schoolteacher.

Miss K. smiled and said, "Yep those are my boys."

Sarah thought about having a whole room full of sons.

Then Miss K. asked, "Did you and your husband do some fucking last night."

Sarah told her, "No."

Miss K. just smiled and said, "Well that relationship is doomed."

The next day Sarah was having a hard shift. She went into Miss K's room and Sarah watched her sleep. It made her feel calm again when she watched the old patients sleep. Then she saw that Miss K. had a visitor and the visitor was sleeping too but then the gray haired man was startled and woke up.

"Oh I'm sorry," Sarah said. "I was just checking on her." Sarah started to leave. "No, stay," the gray haired man said. He must have been only 50 or so. "She likes you and she hardly likes anyone." Then the man in Miss K's room took off his glasses and rubbed his eyes. "I was dreaming we were at the beach and it was years ago. It was before everything got so messed up. I took a picture of her on the balcony of our hotel and she looked beautiful. We sat on that beach and looked out at the ocean and all that rolling water and the moon."

Sarah was confused. What did he mean, "She always looked beautiful at the ocean?" Of course, Sarah thought that this man was just another one of Miss K's sons. He looked so young. But then he told her he was one of her ex-husbands. Sarah said, "Oh well, I wasn't sure she'd been married before. I knew she had sons." The man stopped and told her no. She never had any children. There weren't any sons. The men who had been coming to visit her and take care of her were all her ex-husbands. The man smiled and told Sarah that Miss K. had been married six times.

"Well she must have been an amazing woman," Sarah said. And the man just shook his head. "Yes, she was. We're all still here helping to take care of her." So that night Sarah walked to her car and looked up at the moon and it was the same moon from ten thousand years ago. It was the same moon that everyone looked at from the beginning of time.

Miss K. never made it to the beach again. A week passed and then two weeks passed and then a month and then two months. Miss K. was still in the ICU. She was on the vent the last week of her life. Sarah came home one night and said Miss K. died and she thought it was the strangest death she'd ever witnessed. I asked her why it was so strange. Sarah thought about the people who she lost. Then she saw her father. He was sick and she couldn't help him. She saw her mother and she was sick and Sarah couldn't help her. Sarah saw her own children sick and she couldn't help them. Sarah said Miss K's death was so strange because there was so much love in the room. She said all of the husbands who were still living stood by her bed and they gathered around the bedside and then one by one they stooped and said goodbye. Some were crying and some whispered I love you and held her and touched her forehead and kissed her cheek. And then Miss K. who had not moved in weeks looked as if she was smiling and the men all held hands around her bed.

They held hands and swayed and the former husband who had been a preacher shouted, "Hallelujah." It was not a day of sorrow. It was a day of joy. And they would all be going home soon. Then he broke up and said. "Go away sweetheart, where we are all young and still in love." Then Miss K. raised her arms into the air and Sarah wished for a thousand husbands. Sarah wished for ten thousand husbands, and they were all singing love songs for her and she saw a million husbands surrounding her and they were all wanting her and waiting on her. They were all waiting for her love.

A few months later Sarah heard a story about Miss K's ex-husbands. She heard they were all still living in Miss K's house together. There were only three of them now but they were all there. They were together and they were all taking care of one another now. It made them feel close just to be around the things she loved.

I n the coming years, Sarah continued to watch the things she loved grow older and die. It started when Mr. King stopped walking. In the evenings he lay at my feet and our other dog Bertie came over and licked his eyes. She was his sister.

Bertie licked the empty socket that was missing the eyeball and then she licked the eye that was blind. She licked the black juice that oozed from the empty eye-socket and she licked King's ears that always had a strange odor and a brown fluid.

Then she licked the eye socket again and King breathed heavy and then excited and then sleepy and then he yawned and you could see inside his mouth and the few teeth he had left. But then he would whine sometimes. Whine about how dark the world was and it was like he was scared of the dark now.

But his sister was giving him a bath.

"Aww," Sarah said. "That's sweet."

I told her that it wasn't affection we were seeing but just something salty on King's coat that tasted nice and we mistook it for love. Mistakes. He said she said bullshit. But then Sarah said that maybe even ants feel life and we just can't communicate with them.

I laughed and told her we were all animals licking empty eye sockets.

Finally one night I said that it was getting to be time and that we needed to put Mr. King down. I told her that he'd lived a long life but he was just suffering now.

Sarah asked me how he was suffering because she still thought he was the happiest animal she knew.

"He just likes sitting and being," she said.

"That's because he's blind," I told her.

But Sarah said he'd suffered so much in his life and that I was just jealous because I still thought she loved him more. She told me she just wanted to give him more time in this world and she wanted to give him more time to enjoy his love and his treats.

I told her that his teeth had fallen out and he couldn't really enjoy anything because he didn't have teeth.

But I agreed to let him live.

In the mornings I still picked him up and took him outside to piss and at noon I took him outside to piss and shit if he hadn't shit in the house yet and then I'd take him outside in the afternoon to piss and shit and then at night I took him out to piss some more. But now he was using the bathroom inside. All of the time. Accidents. Then one night we looked over and he was sleeping and there was shit coming out of him. The house stunk. The shit kept pushing out of him like a giant shit worm and he didn't even know or realize.

He was sleeping.

So we ran around.

I cleaned him up and then a few minutes later it happened again. The wet shit balls dropped from his ass and flopped against the hardwood floor like cookie dough. I had to take him outside.

My father-in-law was visiting from Virginia. Elphonza.

He sat on the cold porch and chewed a piece of Nicorette gum and watched me wipe King's ass with a paper towel and I sprayed King's ass with the water hose.

King had a look on his face like, "Is this the end? Perhaps this is the end for me. I was born a long time ago, but it doesn't seem so long ago now."

I looked at my father-in-law who'd just lost his girlfriend Dagmar to a brain tumor. He showed me a picture of her from a few months before she died and I didn't recognize her. Her head was swollen up like a rotten melon with eyes made of only slits.

The eyes looked like cuts.

Her head was the size of her body almost.

"The steroids swelled her up like that," he said. Then he handed me his phone and I looked at the picture. He said, "Life is something, ain't it?"

I looked at her head and it was swollen up and her face was swollen up and who would have known that when she was a baby she was snuck across the German border and hid from the Nazis inside of a suitcase. Her mother made her drink so much schnapps that her father thought she would die. They made her drink the schnapps so that she would be unconscious and sleeping and she wouldn't cry.

"You're going to kill her," her father told her mother. "She's just a baby."

"We're already dead," her mother said as the baby screams grew less and less and then her infant was asleep. In the picture Elphonza showed me, Dagmar's head looked like a rotten pumpkin and she had that same look on her face like Mr. King. Both pictures said, "Is this the way it's going to end for me? "

I finished cleaning up King and I came inside and I cried. I told Sarah again that King needed to be put down. Sarah cried too but she begged me for another week. And so in this last week, Sarah tried to make the last days of Mr. King wonderful. For years we said Mr. King was immortal and we didn't really know his true age. We imagined him in History Channel documentaries with Alexander and his Macedonians. We imagined him with Hannibal and his Carthaginians. We imagined him in the future with aliens. We imagined him 256 years old. Sarah made him hamburger steak and she let me feed him beer without getting mad. Mr. King and I partied well into the night each night and I told him about my life and how I met the woman who was his final mother. In the mornings Sarah took him on rides and she did his favorite thing. She just sat with him on her lap for hours and rubbed him. He purred and cooed and she held him like a baby.

Mr. King was her baby.

So King slept in her arms like a giant fat baby and there was a look on his face that said, "Perhaps this is not the end. Perhaps this is only a beginning."

But by the end of the week it was all different. He couldn't walk at all now or even really crawl on his front legs. Then one afternoon Sarah and I watched him pull himself around the room on his front paws and drag his dead body behind him. Sarah wanted to pretend that it wasn't happening, but then I noticed something being left behind as he dragged himself.

I picked up Mr. King from the floor and I saw what it was. It was all over my hands and my arms and my shirt.

It was blood.

He'd rubbed his hip raw from the dragging and so I told Sarah it was time to call the vet. The next morning she did.

Sarah cried when she told Mr. King goodbye. She told him she hoped that he was able to find some comfort in his final days and she told him she was sorry if her soft heart made him suffer more. She told him he was a good boy with the sweetest heart she had ever known and then she kissed him and hugged him and then she went away and shut the door to the bedroom behind her.

I heard her crying.

Our other dog, Bertie Mae McClanahan was outside on the chain when she said her goodbye to the strange dog who couldn't see and who was afraid of the dark. She sat and looked up at what once were his sad eyes and I put King in front of her. Then she licked the sockets of his sick eyes for the last time.

Then Bertie's eyes looked to me and she said, "It's a lonely world Scott McClanahan. Why do we have to lose things?" I didn't answer.

I took Mr. King to the car and put him inside and then I drove the few minutes to the vet. I let him out and he did something he loved for the last time. He went over to the grass at the corner of the parking lot and he raised his leg and pissed. His face smiled like he was saying that was the most amazing piss he ever took and then he said, "Isn't pissing fun?" I told him pissing really was fun and then I took him inside the vet's office. Mr. King sat in my lap but he was quiet now. There was a little girl there and she looked at Mr. King. She couldn't have been more than six and she said, "That dog looks funny. He looks old."

I told her he was old.

The little girl asked how old he was and I told her this. I said, "His name is Mr. King and you might not believe it but he is 256 years old."

Then the little girl laughed and said, "No he's not. He's more like 500 years old."

She laughed and I laughed and I watched the little girl keep looking at his eye. Then she asked, "How come his eye is missing? How come he's blind?"

I looked down and said, "Oh my god. His eye is missing? I always wondered why he couldn't see. Thanks for telling me."

She laughed again and then I told her I guess Mr. King saw too much.

Then it was time to go back and see the vet. I said goodbye to the little girl and walked away. The vet asked me how everything was and I told her. Then the vet looked sad and asked me if I wanted to stay. I told the vet that I did and I wanted to be with him in his last moments and Sarah made me promise. The vet gave him a few pets and said, "Well he lived a good long life."

Then she had the needle and then she was filling it full. I kept petting King and talked to him. I said inside my head, "Don't be afraid, Mr. King. Don't be afraid." I was talking to myself.

But in the end Mr. King was afraid. I want to tell you now that he was peaceful and he just closed his eyes and went to sleep. I want to tell you he just went away. I want to tell you he licked my hand to show he loved me. But he didn't. He died like this.

The vet placed the needle in his hide and King panicked. He thrashed around. He shook his head and was so strong that he almost came off the table. I tried holding him down the best

I could but the vet had to call for her assistant who came in and held him down as well. The vet pushed the needle in and Mr. King rose up on his front legs and whipped his head around. Then he did something else. He tried to bite me. He was blind so he couldn't see what he was biting at and then he fell to the table and started shaking from a seizure. He clamped down on his tongue and then his life was gone from him. There was blood coming from his tongue and there was a bile foaming around his lips and there was something oozing from his eye.

I sat with him for a while and the vet asked if I wanted to take him home or if I wanted them to dispose of him and I told the vet that I wanted him. They put him inside of a giant black plastic bag and then they placed him inside of a white box. They gave me the white box and I made a mistake. I left and instead of going out the side door I went back out through the waiting room in the front of the vet's office. The girl was still there and she looked up at me.

"Where is the blind dog?"

I didn't say anything. She looked at the white box and she knew.

Then a vet assistant came out and said, "Sir, the children. Please go out the side door," I was already on my way out the front though. So I put him in the trunk and then I came back inside and paid the 35 dollars it cost for them to stop his life.

I took him home and Sarah was standing in front of the glass door on the porch. When she saw me she buried her face in her hands and ran back inside. I put Mr. King and Mr. King's box under the dogwood tree and then I went inside. Sarah walked back and forth in the kitchen and I couldn't understand what she was trying to say.

I heard her say, "Is he gone?" Then, "Where is he at? Where is he at?"

I showed her. She looked outside the door beneath the dogwood tree.

And then she whined. "How? How, Bubbies?"

I told her he went peaceful and I told her he just went to sleep. I told her he didn't feel a thing. He didn't whine from his fear of the darkness but kicked his legs like he was running. Like he could finally see again. Like he was free.

Sarah wiped the snot from her nose and it was on her cheek now. It hung there and I wiped it away. She gave me his favorite piss smelling blanket and she gave me one of his baby dolls and she gave me some treats. I walked outside and the white box was shining beneath the dogwood tree. The white blossoms from the tree were falling around him and I put the things Sarah had given me inside the box and then I took the box down over the hill. I buried the things inside of the box, but it was so hot that I started sweating and getting tired of digging. My arms ached from the shovel and every time I stabbed the shovel in the ground it felt like stabbing concrete.

I finally quit.

I said, "Surely to god that's deep enough."

Then I preached his eulogy. I told him that God shows us love through our suffering, but we're just living things and can't understand it. I told him that our suffering is a hug from God and one day we would understand, but then I stopped and told him I was sorry because I didn't believe in God.

Then I left his hole in the ground and the days passed. And we didn't talk about King anymore. The house stopped smelling of urine, but then one day I decided to go see. It was a month after and I went to go check on the grave. I walked down over the hill and through the bushes and the briars and the weeds.

I saw that the ground was washed away.

There had been a bunch of water runoff and something was wrong now since I buried him at the bottom of the hill next to a culvert and a swamp. Mr. King was no longer buried and the grave was open and washed out. There was a mushy box there but Mr. King's body had come out of it. I could see his rotting hide coming out of the black bag and his red piss smelled blanket looked rotten as well. I gagged from the smell.

The death smell was a mix of a sweet smell like licorice and something else. Something from the dark. I closed the bag and put him back in the ground and it felt like a bag full of wet towels. So I reburied him. I wondered if maybe this was something other than the ground washing away. I wondered if this was Mr. King resurrecting from the earth and perhaps he had willed it so. After I reburied him, I put a giant boulder over the grave to show me where he was. I returned a few months later and the same thing had occurred. Except this time the stone had been rolled away. The grave was open yet again and the body of Mr. King was gone and perhaps he had resurrected. Or perhaps he'd just been drug away by wild animals in the night. And this is what happens to the helpless things of this world.

That night I dreamed we were all magnets. I dreamed all living things were magnets and from the moment of our births we were being drawn together by some invisible force. I was a magnet and Sarah was a magnet and books were magnets too. We had finally found one another.

In those last days I thought, "What am I going to do?" I didn't want to tell my parents about the divorce date being set because I didn't want to hurt them. I was still telling them we were just separated and everything was going to be okay. I drove over to my Mom and Dad's house with the kids one weekend and tried to figure out what to do. One night Sam woke up at 2 A.M. and I couldn't get him to go back to sleep. I sang to him and then I gave him a bah bah but he wouldn't sleep. I told him, "This is how little guys get shaken baby syndrome, dude." Sam didn't laugh though and just looked up at me with a face like "That's not something to be joking about, fat boy." I rocked him some more and touched his forehead like I was a baby whisperer. Then he just started to smile and giggle and still the baby wouldn't go to sleep. He looked up at me like "What are you going to do? You're so fucked." I told myself that he was just a baby and he couldn't even talk, but I kept imagining he could.

I took Sam and went into the bathroom and I sat him down on the cold floor next to the toilet. Then I sat down on my knees and I started to gag. I put my hands on the toilet seat and Sam just watched me. But then my gag gagged so loud that Sam started to cry. I patted Sam on the back and said, "Daddy's just having a panic attack. Don't worry. Daddy's going to get his shit together I promise." I whispered hush now, but Sam wouldn't stop crying. I tried talking to him and said, "Come on, Sam. Are you a baby or are you a man?" Sam looked at me with his brown eyes and said, "I'm a baby." Then he cried some more. I tried to calm him and reminded myself that this wasn't really Sam talking and he was only one year old. I could hear him judging me and saying, "You even picked up a hitchhiker the other day when you were alone and got drunk with him."

I told him there was nothing wrong with picking up hitch-hikers. I told him what my mom would say, "It could have been Jesus." Then I told him what the hitchhiker said, "It ain't no sin if you've been drinking gin." But Sam wasn't buying it. I turned back to the toilet and I started to throw up a black bile. It dropped in the toilet and sounded like someone clapping hands and then I watched it float on the surface and drift somewhere and seeing it made me more sick. Then: the vomit laughed. Then Sam and the vomit laughed together. They said, "What are you going to do, fat boy? You're totally fucked." Then Sam had a look on his face like, "I hope I get a new stepdad soon. One who doesn't have panic attacks and is rich. I'll probably even change my name to my stepdad's name. Get me a cool ass last name. McClanahan is such a shit name. Get me a rich stepdad. Get me a BMW."

I wiped off my mouth and leaned back against the wall. I told him a good name is chosen rather than great riches.

I heard a knocking at the door. It was my mom. I listened to the knocking and my mom said, "Are you okay, Scott?" She was using the voice she always used when I was 13 years old and I locked myself in the bathroom with the Sears catalog. "Are you okay in there and why did you take the Sears catalog with you?" I couldn't tell her that the bra section had changed my life and I had a purpose now. I couldn't tell her that the bra section had made my life magical. And now it was twenty years later and my mom was still saying, "Are you doing okay in there?" Sam had a look on his face like she's going to find out. Then Mom said, "Are you getting sick in there?" I heard my 13 year old boy voice say from somewhere far away. "No. Mom. God. Leave me alone."

But I didn't. Instead I said, "Yes" and she opened the bathroom door and walked in wearing her nightgown and robe. She looked so much older now. Her hair didn't even have gray anymore. It was white. She'd spent her life watching me grow older, but I'd spent my life watching her grow older too. I got up and gagged in the toilet. She put her arms around me and said, "What's wrong, Scott? What's going on?" Then she picked Sam up and held him against her soft granny chest. She was a momma bear. Then she sat down beside me on the floor and I felt ashamed. I cried and punched the tears away from my eyes with the bottom parts of my hand. Then I told her I was a thorn tree in the whirlwind. I laughed because I didn't know what that meant and she whispered, "What? Tell me, Scott. Tell me." And so I told her that Sarah and I had signed the papers already and the divorce date was set. I told her Sarah said she hadn't loved me in over two years.

My mother watched her child who was now a man look at her and cry. And now—she could do nothing. My mom held Sam and rocked him in her lap and she said she knew there was something going on. She told me the last time she saw Sarah—Sarah looked at her like it was the last time. I listened and Mom asked me if I'd tried everything.

I told her I'd just been giving her space. But I kept hearing the Sam voice in my head and it said, "He called her Dad the other night. Hah. What a pathetic pussy." But then I saw that Sam's face was sleeping now and so he wasn't saying anything and I was losing my shit. I stared at my mom's feet and these were the same feet from long ago. This was something we could always recognize when time had taken its toll. Our dumb feet. She still painted her toenails the same way she did when I was a boy and Sam still wasn't talking and had turned into a baby again. I told Mom I called Elphonza because I didn't know what to do and I wanted to see if he could help me change Sarah's mind. Mom asked me what he said and I said, "He told me I just needed to take care of myself." Then my mom listed off her complaints. She told me I was gruff and hard to get along with and then in her mother voice she told me all of the other things that were wrong with me. She told me I wasn't smarter than god and I told her this was true.

I started to hyperventilate and go "Hee hee ho ho, hee hee ho ho," like I was birthing a baby. I turned to the toilet and gagged gah but Sam was startled with a surprise and opened his eyes. Then he slept some more. I leaned back on my knees and my mom reached around me and did a kind thing. She pushed the handle of the toilet down and I watched it flush. The water twirled in a tornado and I watched it disappear. Then the water filled back up in the toilet again and I leaned back against the wall and cried. I said, "I just love her so much mom. I love her so much." My mom reached out and touched my hand and she said the only thing she could say, "Of course you do, Scott." Then she touched my face and we were taken back in time. I said, "What am I going to do, Mom?" I said it like a man who had no memory and who had forgotten things.

I had forgotten my mom had taught children for 33 years until she became a child herself. She looked at me like a fool, "What are we going to do?" She knew what we were going to do. She said, "First, go to sleep. Go in the bedroom and try to sleep. Second, I'll stay up with Sam for the night."

"And then tomorrow?" I said. "Tomorrow," she said. "Who knows?"

Mom handed me Sam and I held him. He was halfway sleeping still. Then she tried to get up off the floor. "Ugghh, it's no fun getting old," she said. She tried to push herself up on one knee, but it wasn't working. I pushed on her butt and tried to help her and then I stared at the back of her legs and her veins were broken purple and black and blue. She got up on all fours and sat with her butt towards me and then she stood up the way a toddler stands up when she's taking her first steps. She turned towards sleeping Sam and said, "Grandma doesn't move around as good as she used to, Sam. She's getting old." Then she stood up and took the baby back from me and then she told me our plan again. She told me to go to sleep and she would sit with Sam in the living room.

I went into the bedroom and I tried to sleep. I put the pillows over my head and I tried. I turned on the tiny fan my mother kept in the corner to drown out the sounds the house made. Then I closed my eyes and I imagined them in the living room. My mother is sitting in the dark room and rocking Sam. I hear her singing little songs she sang to her first graders long ago, "The Itsy Bitsy Spider" and, "Feed the Birds." She was 63 years old and I needed her again. We were raising children together.

I was late the morning of my divorce hearing because I was writing Sarah a love letter. Of course, I'd been telling her for months now that no one would love her like I did. She always laughed and said, "Thank god. I sure fucking hope not." On the morning of the divorce hearing I got up and wrote her, "I know you said that I never wrote you love letters anymore, but I'm going to try and make up for it. One day I'll write a beautiful book full of pain and laughter." I finished the letter and hit send and imagined her reading it and changing her mind. I got dressed in the same suit I wore at our wedding and I put on the same tie I wore at the wedding too. When I got to the courthouse I could see that Sarah had been crying.

I told her I sent her an email and she said "What?"

I told her I sent her an email and I wondered if she got it. She said she saw it.

I wanted to ask her what she thought of the letter in it, but I didn't. We just sat in the waiting room of the courthouse in Beckley, West Virginia and Sarah saw an old woman in the hallway. The old woman said, "Sarah! I haven't seen you in years." It was Sarah's old babysitter from decades before. Sarah said, "Hi."

Then the old babysitter said, "Well, how have you been and what have you been doing?"

Sarah smiled and said, "Oh you know. I'm here getting a divorce." Then Sarah laughed and then I laughed. The babysitter just stood with her mouth open but then she laughed too. Sarah pointed to me and said, "I might be bad off but at least I'm not as bad off as him. He keeps threatening to take his life and I think he's serious." The former baby sitter didn't know what to say. Sarah and I thought this was normal conversation for the time and I nodded my head yes and smiled because it was true. Then the babysitter told Sarah it was nice seeing her and walked away.

I wanted to ask Sarah if she read my letter and liked it, but I didn't. I just held out my arms and I showed her my wedding suit. I asked her if she recognized the suit.

Sarah said, "Yeah. The worst day of my life."

Then we both laughed and then the bailiff called for us. Before we went inside, I watched Sarah lean into the corner and cry and the bailiff burped a soft burp. He looked at me and I looked at him. I patted Sarah on the back and she put a wadded up tissue to her face. I kept patting Sarah on the back and she finally looked up at me and pulled the tissue away from her nose. She had snot on her face. I was going to reach down and wipe it off but I didn't know if I should. I remembered we were getting a divorce and it's the tiny victories like not wiping off someone's snot that makes life meaningful. I watched a young couple leaving the office of the justice of the peace. They had just been married and they were smiling. They were dreaming about their future together and they were full of joy.

We went inside the courtroom and stood at our separate podiums. I tried not getting mad or reminding her about how she asked the bailiff to move me during our child parenting class. Then the bailiff asked us to raise our hands and we did. He asked us to swear to tell the truth, the whole truth, and we did. Sarah raised her hand but then she had to wipe her nose because she was crying. She dropped her arm and then she wiped her nose some more and then she raised her arm back up. She held it there. Everyone smiled and Sarah said she was sorry. Then we were sworn and we all sat down. The bailiff asked to rise again and the judge came into the room. He told us to be seated and we took our seats. He read our names and then he started talking in talk that sounded like blah blah blah blah blah blah.

The judge started asking us questions. He asked one question and Sarah said yes and he asked another question and Sarah said no. He asked a question and then I said yes and he asked another question and I said no. Then he asked me another question and I said yes when I should have said no and it was obvious to everyone that I should have said yes. So I said yes and then everyone laughed. The judge asked Sarah if she was currently pregnant and Sarah said no. It was some strange antiquated law.

The judge went through the list of the property. He asked both of us if we were happy with the way things were divided and then he asked Sarah if she wanted anything back and Sarah shook her head no. I wasn't crying like Sarah was and I figured this probably impressed the judge. Then he discussed the children and the custody issues. He read the names of the children. Iris McClanahan. Born 6-24-08. And Samuel McClanahan. Born 12-31-10. When he read off the names of the children it was like he was reading the names of hostages. Maybe he was.

He read some more and Sarah started to cry more. This time a deputy brought over a box of tissues and I just stood there. Sarah took a tissue and said "Thank you." Someone else was wiping away her tears now and so I looked over and I saw Sarah's head dropped down and O if I could only tell you how sad Sarah looked. Even now I can see her head bowed. I shake my head but this memory won't turn loose. The judge gave his final verdict. He said my name: Scott McClanahan. He said her name: Sarah McClanahan. And then it was done. When we left the courtroom I told Sarah that I wasn't sure if she had the chance to read my letter that morning, but I'd like it if she read it. I sent it to her email. She was still crying some and she said she would. Then we smiled and I gave her a hug and we walked away.

I imagined her reading the love letter later that night and crying. I imagined her listening to the song I sent her too and whispering, "I've lost him. I've lost him." I imagined her re-reading the letter and thinking she'd like to get back with me and that she'd made a mistake. I imagined the song playing at my funeral far away in the future and Sarah sitting somewhere in the back and her eyes full of tears.

That's how it ended. Two weeks passed and Sarah still hadn't said anything about the love letter I sent on the day of the divorce. I sent her a text one night asking her about it again, but she never replied. So one night I logged into her email and I checked her email like some creep. I saw emails from clothing sites, junk email from baby sites, amazon.com offers and tons of emails from discount websites. They were all saying, "If you don't buy you die." And they were all unopened. I scrolled to the bottom and I discovered the love letter I sent her. I saw the song I had sent her too. She hadn't even checked them. And so I laughed because this was life, and a part of mine was over now and nothing exploded and no light was revealed. I hit delete and I laughed. There was no new path and there was no new way. There was no revelation. There was just a stupid ending and a tiny voice saying, that's all. That's all.

I still had my children at least. But they didn't seem to like me much though. They just wanted to hang out with Grandpa. "You're going to find out that Grandpa isn't what he seems," I told them one weekend on the way to Grandma and Grandpa's house in Rainelle. I told them I knew I hadn't been a good dad recently but I was going to do better. I told them we were going to have a great weekend, and then I told them that I was going to be the one who took care of them. So we drove on and Iris said, "Grandpa?" And Sam said, "Grandpa?" I looked into the rear view mirror and nodded my head and told my son Sam. "Yeah we're going to see Grandpa, but you need to learn something. You have to be your own man. You can't be a follower." I said, "Grandpa might seem cool now because you've just known him for a couple of years, but I've known him for

34 years and he can be a real hard ass sometimes." They weren't even listening to me.

We pulled up and Grandpa was waiting on us. "Grandpa, Grandpa," they shouted. And so Grandpa got Sam out of his car seat and I got Iris out of her car seat. Then Iris demanded for Grandpa to hold her. So Grandpa held Sam and Iris together in his arms and walked to the house. "Little kiss asses," I thought. They went inside the house and Grandpa took them both. Then Sam did what he always did. He demanded to be held upside down. So Grandpa had Sam climb up on his big belly mountain and then he got a hold of Sam's ankles and he flipped him upside down like Sam was a gymnast. Then he started holding Sam upside down and he looked like this:

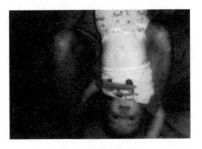

Then Sam did what he always did. He started waving hello at everybody.

Dad stood and Sam swayed back and forth and upside down. And then he did this with Iris and then Sam said, "Upside down. Upside down." Dad started getting tired. He gently put Sam back down on the carpet and then Sam popped back up and said, "Again. Again."

I sat on the couch and I told Mom, "I don't know if that's a good idea."

Mom said, "Oh it's good for them. They like it."

So I just took it. I knew I hadn't been doing a good job. There was the weekend I couldn't get out of bed because I was so depressed. There was the weekend I started weeping when I tried to say grace. There were the weekends I disappeared from our home for hours at a time to drink in the Kroger parking lot. But I was going to do better now. I looked at Sam hanging upside down except now he was doing something else. He was eating potato chips.

I told Grandma even though my dad was standing right there. "I don't think Sam should be eating potato chips and hanging upside down."

But Grandma said, "Well you know your dad, Scott? He just loves them so much and a little potato chips won't hurt them."

But they wouldn't stop doing it. Iris giggled and smiled and swayed during her upside down time, but then she got tired of it. But Sam got so into it that Grandpa got tired and my dad tried to put Sam down. But Sam just kept begging him. "Me. Me. Again. Again."

"Now Grandpa's getting tired," Grandpa repeated, but Sam kept begging. So Grandpa decided to sit down on the couch and hold Sam upside down. This way Grandpa could put his elbows on his knees and then he could hold Sam upside down without getting tired. Sam just hung and swung all possum style and they did it for ten minutes. Then they decided to see if Sam liked hanging upside down for a half hour. "I don't know if we should be doing it that long guys," I said but they didn't listen to me. I wanted to say, "I'm the one who is supposed to be taking care of everybody. I'm the one who is supposed to be playing with them." I tried to play with Iris but she had decided to read a book with Grandma. I kept telling myself it was okay.

I watched my son Sam watch television upside down. I watched him take his juice upside down too and take a big gulp. Then I thought about the original Sam, my friend Sam who I named my son after. I used to drive to Illinois and get drunk with the original Sam in the alleys of Chicago before we read our stories to people in bars. One day we were drinking 40 ounces before our reading and we saw this stray dog pass us. The dog looked at us and we looked at the dog. Then my friend Sam waved at the dog. He waved hello. The dog nodded its head hello. My friend Sam wasn't waving to be funny. He was waving because the dog was alive and we were alive too and we had all met somewhere in this city of Chicago and it was our pain that made us the same. Rich and poor and strangers. We would all be the same one day. Later at the reading I passed out pictures of Iris' sonogram pictures. I told the audience I wanted everyone to hold my child even though they'd never met her— even though she wasn't born yet. And now I looked at both of the children and this memory seemed so long ago and lost in another life that was gone.

My son Sam was hanging upside down and his whole face was getting red and purple and he was watching TV. "Okay guys, we should probably stop," I repeated but nobody listened to me. My father's forearm muscles twisted and tightened until they looked like thick ropes beneath his arm skin. "You okay, dude?" my dad asked and Sam just took another gulp from his upside down juice and giggled. I'd had about enough. I said, "Okay we're cutting this crap out. It's about bed time. We need to brush our teeth." My dad sat Sam down on his back and told him that we needed to get ready to brush our teeth. Sam was upset and hopped right off of his back and ran over to Grandpa's legs and begged. More. More. Grandpa told him he needed to settle down.

Sam's face twisted upside down and full of pain. Then the tears started. They popped out of his eyes like cobra venom spit. I found myself getting pissed off. Then Sam started squealing. I told Sam he could throw a fit all he wanted to but I wasn't going to listen to it. And then I told him Grandpa couldn't save him. I told him I was the one taking care of him and he needed to be a good boy. Not a bad boy. He cried in my father's arms, "Grandpa."

Then I left the room so I wouldn't keep halfway shouting. I helped Iris brush her teeth in the bathroom and I heard my father try to stop Sam from crying. Sam finally stopped crying and he asked my dad to do it again but my dad refused. They were both quiet for a moment and then I heard my dad say like he was a wise man, "It's okay Sam. Your Dad is right. You can't live your life upside down." So I stood in front of the mirror with Iris and I watched her brushing her teeth and it was like I realized something. "He's right. You can't live your life upside down." And then there was another voice inside of my head that said, "Oh, but sometimes you can try."

That night I went into the bedroom where Iris and Sam and I all slept in the same bed together. I tucked them in and I said, "Okay guys. We've had a good day today. So let's all go off to dreamland now." Grandma tucked them in and kissed them goodnight and said, "Let's go off to dreamland." And Grandpa kissed them goodnight and said, "Okay, let's go off to dreamland now." Then they left and I turned off the lights and we went to bed. I didn't tell them a bedtime story or even offer to tell them a story because what could I have told them about but loneliness.

So the three of us crowded in the bed together. Then I got up and started to say what I always said. But Iris beat me to it. She said, "I'll be right back." And so I didn't get to say, "I'll be right back." I just walked to the foot of the bed and I sat on the floor. I opened up my backpack and pulled out my water bottle full of gin. I took the first sip and then I felt my mouth and lips sting. Then I took another sip. My mouth was going numb. Then I heard Iris pop up and say, "I want a snack. I want a snack."

I said, "Shhhh." I told her it was time to go to sleep. I told her it was time for bed. Then Sam said, "Upside down." I told Sam, "Shhhh." I told him it was time to sleep. Then I drank from the water bottle of gin and then Sam sat up and pulled the blankets around him and kept repeating, "Upside down. Upside down."

Iris said, "I want a snack."

I said, "Shhh." I watched their faces in the light that was coming from the window. I saw Sarah and I saw the children. Then Iris and Sam shouted I want a snack and upside down. I stood up and I got back in bed. I told them to shut the hell up. I told them to shut the fuck up and I told them to shut up again. I rested beside them and then I started to cry. I said, "Shut the fuck up" but no one was listening to me. Iris put her hand on my shoulder and she patted me like I was one of her baby dolls. I buried my face and told them how much I loved them and I cried against her side like I was her child.

I closed my eyes and I imagined that I was a baby and I was being hung upside down and I imagined that if I had a goodnight story to tell them it would go like this: We are all babies and we are all being held by an invisible force and we are all eating potato chips. We are waving like Sam waves and our faces are turning red. We are all waving so desperately hello.

The next morning I sat on the couch with Sam and Iris and I read There's a Monster at the End of this Book. I remembered reading it from my own childhood. In the book Grover kept warning the reader that there was a monster at the end of the book and not to turn the page. Iris and Sam laughed as we turned the page.

Grover built walls and he set fires and did all kinds of things to keep us from turning the page.

But of course, we kept turning the page. He kept begging and pleading please. Don't turn the page. Please don't turn the page. I told the kids, "The best thing about books is you can turn back and start all over. You can turn back to page five and the people will still be here inside of the pages. Alive." But then I remembered life wasn't a book.

I could see right then that I was just like Grover and I wanted everyone to stop turning the page.

I wanted to say, "The end is coming. There's a monster at the end of this book and it's you and me. It's how everything changes." I wanted to say, "Please don't turn the page. The end is here."

A few nights later I was all alone in the apartment of death. I sat for awhile on the bed and wondered what I should do. I took off all of my clothes and walked to the dresser. I pulled out the pair of women's underwear I had kept from long ago. I put one leg through and then I put another leg through. I felt parts of myself fall from around the sides of the underwear. This is what I always did when I was lonely. I took the lipstick that I had from an old travel bag when I moved from Sarah's house. I slipped off the top and put it on. I took the blush and I popped the top open. Then I put on the blush. I blended and blended. I took out all of the old pictures from the drawer and I put them in front of me. I saw pictures of Sarah and pictures of me and all of the people I loved. I looked at their faces now and I knew that I was each of them. I opened the mascara and I tapped it against the bottom lash tap. I saw that my face was every face. I walked to the mirror and I looked at myself. I stared into my eyes now and I whispered my new name. My name was the past.

A lmost two years passed before I saw Sarah again, but then one day everyone decided to get together. We were both re-married now and I didn't know what we were going to talk about though. For the past year and a half we communicated through texts and we communicated through the babysitter who dropped the kids off at my apartment and then picked them back up when the weekend was over. "I'm so fucking nervous I think I'm going to have a panic attack," Julia said as we sat in the parking lot of the hamburger place. I was nervous about it too, but I told Julia not to worry about it.

I told Julia that maybe Sarah would tell us a story and make us laugh. Maybe she'd tell us about the patient who got his dick amputated. He was this old man who came in with a two liter bottle stuck around his penis and his dick was all black and swollen up inside. His wife said he peed in a bottle at night because he was frail and sick, but then one night he fell asleep and when he woke up his penis was all swollen inside of the bottle. They were too embarrassed to call the ER. They waited for two days and the dick tissue had died inside the bottle. They had to amputate half of his dick and I told Julia that maybe Sarah would tell us that story.

Julia just laughed at me and told me she was still nervous. I took my hands and put them on Julia's chest and then I grabbed the nervous energy in fistfuls and threw it off of her and on the floor. Then Julia did the same for me. She took handfuls of my nervous energy and threw it all away. And so we waited and I texted Sarah because I still didn't see them. Sarah texted back. "O we're already here. We're outside." Julia and I got out of the car and I said, "I have no fucking idea what we're going to talk about." Then we walked to the side of the restaurant where everybody was sitting. There was Sarah and there was Dr. Jones and there were the kids. Sam and Iris had quiet faces of surprise. I said, "Hey everybody." Then Sam started jumping straight into the air jump jump like he was trying to catch something. I said, "Sam, what are you trying to do buddy?"

Sam pointed up to an airplane in the sky and said some shit I couldn't understand. Then Sarah laughed and said, "O he's trying to catch airplanes."

We stood and watched Sam trying to catch airplanes out of the sky. We all laughed nervous and then I shook Dr. Jones' hand and said, "Hello." Then Julia did the same. I walked around the table and I gave Sarah a hug and then she said,

"Hey skinny." I said, "Hey, old girl." But then I stopped and said, "I'm sorry. I'm sorry. I didn't mean 'old' I just meant…" Sarah laughed and said, "No, you're right. We are old." Then Julia shook Sarah's hand and we all sat down. I looked at Sarah and I kept thinking she looked different or something. Like she'd lost things too. Sarah wrote down what everyone wanted and went to the counter and ordered and paid. Dr. Jones kept saying to Sam. "Daddy's here. It's daddy." Sam smiled. Dr. Jones kept saying "Daddy" and making sure I heard it

I kept thinking about what the fuck we were going to talk about. So we sat at the table and Sarah came back and passed out the big bag of food. The bag wrinkled and the french fry grease soaked through the sides in little circles of grease spots. Then Sarah gave Iris some fries and some chicken nuggets. Then Sarah gave Sam his hamburger and fries. Sarah said, "Be careful now. Because it's hot. Hot." Then Sarah pointed to something behind us all and said, "Baby, would you get Iris a lid?" So I turned in my chair without thinking. And then Jones moved at the same time. I realized I wasn't the baby Sarah was talking to. I was the baby from long ago and she babied a new baby now. I had a new baby too named Julia. I turned back around and looked at Sarah and then Sarah looked at me. Then we looked away together. Then Dr. Jones sat back down and got a lid and put it on top of Iris' drink. I drank my drink and Iris drank her drink and then Iris pointed to my drink and said, "Don't pill it poppa." Then everyone laughed and I whispered to Iris, "I'll try not to pill it little girl if you promise not to pill it too."

Sarah smiled and I smiled and Julia smiled and Jones smiled and we ate our food. And so we sat and I wondered if Sarah was going to tell the story about the guy who got his dick stuck inside the two liter bottle and then fell asleep and woke up with it all swollen and black. But she didn't. I wondered if she was going to talk about how a congestive heart patient's testicles swell up as big as basketball sometimes because the fluid has nowhere else to go. The balls get so big the nurses have to finally prick them with a pin and let them drain.

But Sarah didn't talk about that either. She just kept reaching over and tearing up the little hamburger she bought for Sam and made sure the pieces were bite size. The hamburger pieces were all crushed with thumb prints and then she licked the ketchup from her fingers. I kept saying inside my head, "Why isn't she being funny? You're not being funny at all." I wanted to tell Julia, "I promise you Sarah is much funnier than this in real life. She's usually the funniest." But this was real life. And so we sat and ate and I wondered if Sarah was different or if she'd always been like this and that I was the one who wasn't funny anymore. But we didn't talk about any of this. We didn't talk about water bottles full of gin or burning Bibles or how Mountain Dew would shrink your penis. We didn't talk about destroying computers with sledge hammers or asking for a divorce or saying I love you and I love you no more. We didn't talk about what we were once and how all things merge into one. We didn't talk about first dates or kissing with our eyes open or trying to commit suicide with Tylenol PM. Instead, we just sat and ate hamburgers and we were all so fucking boring now. We didn't have anything to say to one another. We were called a family.

So we all laughed like nothing had ever happened and our gender wasn't pain. I looked at Julia and I looked at Jones and we were all magnets. Then Sam said he was finished and got up and stood beside the table. He stared at the sky until he saw an airplane again and tried to catch it. And we all smiled. I knew one day we would return here after the earth was gone and stare at one another and eat hamburgers and say, "Was it not real? Was it not as it once was." We watched Sam jump and jump some more. I saw Sam and I saw Iris and I saw Sarah and all I could see was Sarah now. Sam was a Sarah and Iris was a Scott and the rivers were a Sarah and the sky was a Sarah and the mountains were a Sarah and Sarah was a Scott. Then I smiled and I saw my face in the window, but my face wasn't my face anymore.

I was a Sarah too.